Across the Lines

CAROLYN REEDER

For my son, David

Many thanks to National Park Service historian Chris Calkins and to Civil War buff Don White for their generous help with historical background and details.

AVON BOOKS, INC.
1350 Avenue of the Americas
New York, New York 10019

Published by arrangement with Atheneum Books for Young Readers, an imprint of Simon & Schuster Children's Publishing Division
Visit our website at **http://www.AvonBooks.com**
Library of Congress Catalog Card Number: 96-31068
ISBN: 0-380-73073-1

First Avon Camelot Printing: December 1998

Printed in the U.S.A.

A NOTE ON THE LANGUAGE AND HEADINGS IN ACROSS *the* LINES

At the time of the Civil War, the word "Negro" was used by northerners, southerners, and people of African descent. The U.S. government, however, used the term "colored," as in United States Colored Troops. "Black" was used descriptively, as in "black people."

Plantation owners rarely used the word "slave." They spoke of their slaves as their Negroes, their servants, their field hands, their people, etc.

Southerners of both races used the titles "aunt" and "uncle" to show respect for elderly slaves and the title "Miss" before the first name of a white woman or girl. Slaves and servants used the title "marse" (master) before a man's or boy's first name.

Northerners spoke of their army as the "Union" army and called the southerners "Rebels."

Southerners called their army the "Confederate" army and called the northerners "Yankees."

The speech of the southern Negroes in *Across the Lines* is patterned after that recorded in oral history interviews of freed slaves (except for substituting "gonna" for the awkward spelling commonly used for the dialect form of "going to") and on linguists' studies of Black English.

When a complete date is used, as in "June 9, 1864," what follows is based on a specific historical event.

→MAY 5, 1864

The two boys raced across the lawn toward the bluff that overlooked the river. Simon was in the lead, but as they neared the oak tree he began to slow, and Edward passed him.

Just once, I'd like to win fair and square, Edward thought as he reached the tree. He grabbed the knotted rope that hung from a high limb, and hand over hand he pulled himself up to the platform he and Simon had built. Kneeling just below the leafy canopy, Edward lifted the field glasses that hung around his neck and trained them on the river. It was true, he thought, and Duncan hadn't been exaggerating, either.

Simon climbed onto the platform and hauled up the rope. "What can you see, Marse Edward?" he asked.

"Yankee ships, and lots of them. Here, have a look."

Duncan's excited voice floated up to the boys' perch: ". . . must be the whole Yankee fleet—look at those ironclads!"

Edward peered down and saw his mother and little sister hurrying across the lawn behind his older brother, with the house servants trailing after them.

Simon handed back the field glasses and Edward trained them on the metal-hulled ships that excited his brother so. Then, hearing band music in the distance, his eyes swept the river until he saw a small boat filled with instrumentalists. Behind it were ships packed rail to rail with blue-clad men.

"Soldiers, too!" Edward exclaimed, his pulse racing. The enemy's fleet and their army, headed toward Richmond, toward the Confederacy's capital. If the Yankees managed to take the city this time, would that be the end of the war? Edward didn't want the South to lose, but he longed to have his father safe at home again.

From the base of the tree Duncan called, "Hey, up there! Toss down the field glasses."

Handing them to Simon, Edward leaned over the edge of the platform and said, "I haven't got 'em." Duncan didn't have any more right to those field glasses than he did, Edward thought. Father had left them behind after his last furlough, and—

"Marse Edward! Look!"

Alarmed by the urgency in Simon's voice, Edward took back the glasses. His mouth went dry when he saw that several of the troop-filled vessels had veered out of line and were headed toward the steamboat landing at the foot of the bluff. He heard agitated voices below him and knew that everyone else was hurrying back to the house, but still he kept his eyes trained on the approaching boats.

Suddenly, Edward's heart almost stopped. *The soldiers that crowded the decks of the boats were Negroes!*

Wild-eyed, he turned to Simon, but Simon was staring toward the lane that led up from the wharf. "Look, Marse Edward!" he said. *"Look there!"*

Edward stared in disbelief. The black Yankee soldiers were swarming up from the landing! He made a dive for the rope and swung off the platform, calling, "Come on, Simon!" He hardly noticed the rough fibers burning his hands as he slid down the rope, and the instant his feet touched the ground, he was racing toward the house.

Edward's heart beat wildly. He felt like he was living the dream he sometimes had—the one where he was running for his life but his movements were as slow as if he were swimming through molasses. It seemed hours before his feet pounded across the veranda and he practically fell through the door his little sister held open for him.

He glanced back and saw that Simon had paused halfway to the house and was looking at the soldiers massed in the lane. "Hurry, Simon!" Edward called, and Simon turned and loped toward him.

"Everybody's packing," seven-year-old Becky said, tugging at Edward's arm. "We're going to Petersburg to stay with Aunt Charlotte."

"What if the Yankees won't let us leave?" Edward asked.

Duncan turned from the window and gave him a withering look. "*Let* us leave? They'll *make* us leave, and with only an hour to pack. Don't you know anything?"

Mother's quick footsteps were on the stairs and Edward heard her say, "But it all *has* to fit in the trunks, Elberta. You'll just have to see that it does. And hurry!" A moment later she saw Edward and cried, "Where on earth have you been? And where's Simon? I need him to help Calvin load the wagon so we can send it on ahead." Her voice was shrill.

"He's right outside, Mother," Edward said.

She brushed by him and called, "Stop gawking at those

Yankees and get yourself out to the smokehouse, boy. Now!"

Still looking over his shoulder, Simon disappeared around the corner of the house. Edward stared after him, puzzled. What had gotten into Simon? He hadn't said "Yes, Miss Emily," and he didn't seem to be in any hurry, either.

Mother's voice broke into Edward's thoughts. " . . . and put it here in the hall. Quickly!"

As he ran up the stairs, Edward's mind raced ahead, planning what he would take with him. By the time he had found his sketch pad and stacked his things in the hall for Elberta to pack, the mule-drawn wagon was at the door.

"I thought Simon was helping you," Edward said as Calvin came in for the trunks.

Calvin shook his head. "I ain't seen dat boy since de mornin'," he complained. "Never can find him when dere's work to be done. Soon's I load dis wagon, den he come 'round."

But when the wagon rumbled off, Simon was still nowhere to be found. Edward burst into the parlor calling, "Simon! Simon, where are you?" He yanked the heavy draperies aside, hoping that the black boy was behind them, but found himself facing only the patterned wallpaper. His body sagged as despair washed over him. He'd searched everywhere—all their favorite hiding places, indoors and out—over and over again. Where could Simon be?

Inside the parlor chimney, Simon concentrated on bracing himself against the sooty bricks. *He won't find me he won't find me he won't find me,* Simon repeated silently. *He won't find me.*

The calls began to fade away, but Simon knew the other boy would be back. Carefully, he shifted his position, trying to ease his aching back and cramped legs. He caught his breath as a piece of soot fell from the chimney into the fireplace below, and he pressed his feet and back against the bricks. Think about freedom, he told himself. Think about being free, like those soldiers in the lane.

Marse Edward was calling him again, and Simon's heart beat faster as the calls grew louder. He congratulated himself for listening to his older brother, Ambrose, and saving this hiding place until he really needed it. For never giving in to the temptation to use it during all the years of playing hide-and-seek with his young master. He heard footsteps in the hall, and his heart pounded so hard he feared it would shake him from his perch.

"Simon?" Edward called, glancing around the parlor again. "*Si*mon!" His breath came in gasps.

Behind him, a deep voice said, "Miss Emily say it time to leave, Marse Edward." He whirled around to face Isaac, the coachman, who added, "Everybody waitin' fo' you in de carriage."

"But I can't find Simon!"

"Simon, he might not want nobody to find him," Isaac said. "Beside, dat Yankee officer say de hour up."

With enormous effort, Edward managed to keep his voice calm. "Tell Mother I'll be right out," he said. But as soon as Isaac turned away, Edward ran to the river entrance where the Yankee officer stood guard. Steeling himself to speak to the Yankee again, Edward asked, "Are you *sure* you haven't seen a Negro boy a couple inches taller than me?"

The young man shook his head. "Told you before, nobody's come out this way." Then he pulled his watch from his pocket and said, "Your hour's up, sonny."

Edward turned away and ran through the hall to the other door. Outside, Isaac waited for him, his ebony face expressionless. Avoiding his eyes, Edward climbed into the carriage, moving a pile of quilts from the seat onto his lap. He carefully placed his sketch pad on top of the quilts, then made room for his feet between a box of papers from Father's desk and the small wooden chest that held the family silver.

Edward stared down at the sketch pad and tried to compose himself. How could this be happening? His fingers almost tingled with his need to draw the Negro soldiers milling about in the lane, to draw the white officer lounging on the veranda while inside the house the frantic family packed. *To draw Simon.*

"I told you you'd never find Simon if he didn't want you to," taunted fifteen-year-old Duncan, grudgingly moving over to give Edward a little more room. "That boy has more hiding places than you can shake a stick at."

The carriage began to roll, and Edward pressed his face against the window, his jaws clenched. He didn't blame Simon for making himself scarce so he wouldn't have to take orders from Duncan, but why would Simon hide from *him?* Especially at a time like this.

As the carriage left the plantation and entered the tiny village of City Point, Duncan broke the silence. "I never did find Father's field glasses."

Edward's heart sank. He must have left them on the tree platform.

"I wouldn't be surprised if Simon took them," Duncan added.

"Simon doesn't take things, and you know it," Edward said, rising to Duncan's bait.

Across from them, Mother said sharply, "We have more important things to worry about than field glasses. Or Simon. I'm not all that sorry he ran off. He'd have been more a burden than a help to us in Petersburg—that boy never did earn his keep."

Ran off? Speechless, Edward stared at his mother. His mind flew back over the past hour and he heard again the excitement in Simon's voice when the Negro soldiers headed for the landing, saw him stop to look back at them in the lane. And then he heard Isaac saying that maybe Simon didn't want to be found.

It was true. Simon had run off. Edward felt Duncan's eyes on him, and he concentrated on keeping his face from showing the mixture of shock and betrayal he felt. It was bad enough to be driven away from Riverview without leaving Simon behind, too.

Simon dropped from his hiding place in the parlor chimney and scrambled out of the hearth. He straightened up, flexed his aching muscles, and wiped his sooty hands on his pants legs. "I'm free," he whispered, hardly believing it. "Free." A feeling of exhilaration swept over him, and he threw back his shoulders and shouted, "I'm free!" The words rang in the empty room.

Peering out the window, Simon saw that the dust had already settled behind the carriage that had carried Marse Edward and the others away. For a moment, his exuberance was dampened. In his dreams of freedom, he'd never thought about leaving Marse Edward. But from the moment he'd seen those Yankee soldiers coming up the lane, all he could think of was that they were black like he was—and they were free.

And now he was free, too! A sense of power surged over Simon and he headed down the wide hall to the door that faced the river. As he stepped outside, his mind began to race. Now that he was free, he could do anything and go anywhere he wanted to. No one could make him work. He could leave the plantation without a pass. He could—

"Well, well! You wouldn't be Simon, would you?"

Simon whirled around. "How'd you know my name?" he asked suspiciously.

The Union officer grinned. "I heard it often enough in the past hour, don't you think? How come you didn't answer your young master when he called you?"

"'Cause I wanted to be free," Simon answered honestly.

"And how are you going to live, now that you're free?"

"Don't know yet," Simon muttered. He hadn't had time to think about that, hadn't planned everything out the way his brother Ambrose had planned *his* flight to freedom. He'd simply seen an opportunity and taken it.

The Union officer looked at him closely and said, "You're well-spoken for a slave."

"Miss Emily, she wanted her sons' servants to talk proper," Simon explained, "an' Marse Edward, he taught me 'most everything he learned from his tutor." Marse

Edward hadn't cared a bit that it was against the law to teach a slave to read.

The officer turned away. "Then I guess I'd better look somewhere else if I want a darky to work for me."

"I'll work for you, sir," Simon said, hurrying after him. He'd always been expected to "talk proper" to white folk, but it looked like Yankees didn't much like that.

The officer paused, looking dubious, and Simon added, "I can take care of your uniforms an' run errands an' do anything else you want me to." That was how he'd live now that he was free—he'd work and earn money to buy whatever he needed. Or wanted.

"I could use someone to fix my meals and tend my horse, too, if you don't think that's beneath you."

"It ain't b'neath me," Simon said quickly.

The officer looked pleased. "That's settled, then," he said. "You'll be my darky, and for your pay, you'll get room and board."

"Beggin' your pardon, sir, but what's that mean?"

"It means that you can bed down in my tent and I'll see to it you get a share of rations. Of food, that is. My name's Lieutenant Hawkins, by the way. You'll call me 'Lieutenant.'"

Subdued, Simon watched the white officer walk away. "Room and board" for his work instead of pay? So far, there didn't seem to be all that much difference between being a slave and being free. He'd rather do for Edward than some stranger, Simon thought, hoping he hadn't made a mistake.

A few miles to the southwest, Edward stared blankly out the carriage window. It had all happened so fast! This morning they were plantation owners with a crew of field hands hard at work growing food for the Confederate army. But now all they had to their names was what they'd managed to bring with them in the carriage, the wagonload of food and clothing Mother had sent ahead, and three faithful Negro servants. Three, when there should have been four.

Edward swallowed hard and gripped his sketch pad more tightly. He wished he could open it to a blank page and lose himself in his drawing, longed for the calm sense of control he always felt as he worked. Drawing was his haven, his escape, but only Simon seemed to understand how important it was to him. *Simon.*

Think about something else, Edward told himself sternly. He focused his attention on Becky, sitting opposite him with her doll cradled in her arms and the box with her treasured china tea set resting on her lap. Her dark curls were tussled, and no one had reminded her to bring her bonnet.

Mother, though, had somehow found time to change into her good dress and bonnet, Edward noticed as he shifted his gaze. If it weren't for the pair of feather pillows and the crystal punch bowl on her lap, she'd look like she was going visiting.

Suddenly, Duncan's voice broke the silence. "There it is—the defensive line," he announced. "Ten miles of fortifications looping around Petersburg," he added with satisfaction, craning his neck for a better look.

As the road passed between two huge banks of earth, Edward gave a sigh of relief. With the swift Appomattox River on the north and an unbroken line of trenches protecting other approaches to the city, they wouldn't have to worry about the Yankees anymore. In Petersburg, they would be safe.

"I'm glad we're going to live in the city with Aunt Charlotte and Mary Beth, aren't you?" Becky said, almost as though she'd read his mind.

"Glad!" Duncan burst out, turning from the window to stare at his sister. "How could anyone be 'glad' to have to be taken in like—like poor relations?"

Ignoring Duncan, Mother said, "I hate the idea of being run off by the Yankees, and *Negro* Yankees at that, but I'd have gone to stay with Charlotte long ago if I hadn't promised your father we'd stay at Riverview."

"So you're glad to leave, too." Duncan sounded scornful.

"I don't deny it will be a relief to let someone else make the decisions for a while," she admitted.

"I'm sure Aunt Charlotte will be quite happy to make all your decisions for you, Mother," Duncan said.

Mother's eyes darkened with anger. "That was uncalled for, Duncan. I don't want to hear any more of your back talk—not now, and not while we're staying with Charlotte. And," she continued, shifting her attention to Edward, "I don't want to hear anything about Simon, either. That boy had far too much influence over you."

"But he was a good influence! He—"

"That's nonsense, and I don't want to hear another word about it," Mother said sharply.

It isn't nonsense, Edward argued silently. Simon had taught him almost everything he knew—not just how to swim and fish, and how to throw with almost perfect aim, but important things, too. Like how to calm himself so he didn't explode with anger when Duncan teased him, and how to keep his expression from showing everything he felt. Because of Simon, his brother no longer tried to make his life difficult. Because of Simon, people no longer could glance at him and read his thoughts.

They rode in silence until Becky exclaimed, "Look, Mama! I can see church steeples—and the courthouse tower."

They were almost there, Edward thought, his eyes moving from the chimney of the gasworks to the smoke that poured from the stacks of the ironworks. He wondered how places less than ten miles apart could be as different as Petersburg and Riverview, their plantation on City Point.

"Look at that!" Duncan exclaimed, and Edward leaned across him to peer at a crowd of men and older boys milling around in a field.

"Those men have guns!" cried Becky, pulling back from the carriage window.

"Word must have reached Petersburg that Yankees have landed at City Point," Duncan said, his voice tense with controlled excitement. "They've called out the citizens to help defend the city."

Edward's chest tightened, and it took all his will to keep from looking back to see if enemy troops were behind them. His apprehension grew when they passed a group of gray-haired civilians hurrying toward the earthworks. It would take more than a few middle-aged businessmen to hold back the hordes of Yankees that had come ashore at City Point.

The carriage rolled into town and finally came to a stop

in a pleasant residential neighborhood. Edward stepped out onto the brick sidewalk and looked at his aunt's house as if he'd never seen it before. Slowly, he followed the others up the stairs to the wide front porch.

Aunt Charlotte was already at the door to greet them, looking solid and comfortable. "I'm so glad to have you all here with us, where you'll be safe!" she exclaimed, hugging each of them in turn. "Calvin and Elberta told me what happened, and I've sent them around back to unload the wagon," she added as she drew them into the house. "Isaac, you can put Miss Emily's punch bowl on the buffet in the dining room," she called over her shoulder to the coachman.

A thin, middle-aged Negro woman appeared in the doorway, a disapproving look on her face, and Edward's heart sank. He'd forgotten about Jocasta. He'd never liked his aunt's servant, and she'd had no use for him since the time years before when he had mistakenly assumed she was a slave. "I'se a free woman," she had said, her eyes blazing. "I works fer wages, an' I can leave dis place anytime it don' suit me." Edward hadn't forgotten that day, and he knew she hadn't either.

Aunt Charlotte turned to the woman and said, "Jocasta, make up Master Wesley's room for the boys and the guest room for Miss Emily." Her plain face softened when she smiled at Becky and added, "We'll put you in with Mary Beth."

Edward wondered what his sixteen-year-old cousin would think about that. He didn't have to guess how Duncan felt about sharing a room with him. If only Wesley and

Duncan could trade places, we'd all three be happier, Edward thought. Wesley could stay home and the two of them could share his room while Duncan went off to fight the Yankees.

Later, as they all sat around the table at suppertime, Aunt Charlotte said, "With prices what they are, your hams and sweet potatoes and those barrels of cornmeal you sent ahead on the wagon are going to come in handy, Emily."

"I wish we could have brought more. After all, you have four more mouths to feed now," Mother said.

"*Seven* mo'," Jocasta muttered as she refilled the water glasses.

Aunt Charlotte said sharply, "That will be quite enough, Jocasta."

"What did she mean?" asked Becky. "Can't she count?"

Edward saw a faint flush of pink creep over his mother's face when she explained, "She's counting Isaac and Calvin and Elberta, too." Then Mother turned to her sister. "Tomorrow I'd like you to help me arrange to rent out my Negroes and sell the horses and mules, Charlotte. Then I'll be able to contribute to our keep."

"Nonsense, Emily! You and the children are our guests," Aunt Charlotte said. But Edward thought he saw an expression of relief flicker across her face. He was relieved, too. Nobody could think you were poor relations if you paid your own way.

THE NEXT DAY

When Edward opened his eyes it took a moment to remember where he was, but then the memory of all that had happened the day before flooded over him. The river full of Yankee boats. The Negro troops landing. Leaving Riverview—and Simon. For as long as he could remember, Simon had always been there—his companion as well as his servant. It felt strange to wake up without Simon there to greet him, without his clothes laid out for him.

The clatter of hooves on the cobblestones outside drew Edward to the window, and he stood looking down at the street. If Simon were here, they could explore the neighborhood together like they used to, he thought, and maybe walk out to take a closer look at those earthworks. "I'll go by myself," Edward muttered.

When everyone had gathered for breakfast, Aunt Charlotte asked, "Well, have you boys decided how you'll spend your first full day in Petersburg?"

"I'm going to join the home guard," Duncan announced.

Becky looked at him, puzzled. "What's that?"

"It's just another name for the reserve militia," Duncan said, reaching for a biscuit.

Becky's frown grew deeper, and Mary Beth explained, "The home guard protects the city just like the militia did before the war started." She turned to Duncan and said, "Wesley was in the home guard before he joined the army."

Edward thought of scholarly Cousin Wesley putting aside his books and going off to fight for the Confederacy, and he was glad that he was only twelve. He was counting on the war being over long before he was old enough to be a soldier.

It was hard for Edward to imagine himself facing the enemy. Facing danger. He knew he'd never *volunteer,* like Father had and like Duncan surely would. Edward still didn't understand why Father had joined the army even though the Confederate government had exempted anyone who owned more than twenty slaves.

"Do you think I could wear Wesley's home guard uniform, Aunt Charlotte?" Duncan asked, his voice eager.

"The home guard doesn't have uniforms, Duncan. It's really nothing more than a group of men and boys who are either too old or too young to be in the army." Duncan's face fell, and his aunt quickly added, "Still, we all rest more easily knowing they're ready to defend Petersburg."

After Duncan had excused himself from the table Mother said, "I do wish you hadn't encouraged him, Charlotte. He's only fifteen, you know."

"I'm well aware of that, Emily, and I didn't encourage him. I simply answered his question."

Edward held his breath, hoping Aunt Charlotte's blunt reply wouldn't make Mother's temper flare. But instead of taking offense, she asked weakly, "Do you think he'll be in any danger, Charlotte?"

"The home guard's been called out now and then, like it was yesterday, but so far nothing's come of it," Aunt Charlotte said. "I wouldn't worry if I were you, Emily."

"But you're *not* me. You're not watching *your* son—"

Mother covered her mouth with her hand. "I'm so very sorry, Charlotte," she said quietly. "I wasn't thinking."

Edward's face burned with embarrassment. How could Mother make such a fuss about Duncan playing soldier here in Petersburg when Cousin Wesley was a real soldier fighting miles from home?

"No harm's done," his aunt said brusquely. She turned to Edward and asked, "What about you? What adventures do you have planned for today?"

"I guess I'll go exploring."

Mother said, "It will be good for you to be on your own for a change instead of going along with whatever mischief Simon could think of." She turned to her sister and added, "Being rid of that lazy boy is the only good that's come out of all this, Charlotte. I wouldn't have sold him, of course, since Edward was so attached to him, but I certainly am glad I've seen the last of that one."

Edward pushed back his chair and stood up. "May I please be excused, Aunt Charlotte?" he asked, fighting to keep his voice steady.

As he passed Jocasta he heard her mutter, "Guess he don' much like it dat his slave boy done cut dat apron string an' gone free." Edward pretended he hadn't heard her and headed for the front door. Apron string, indeed! It was true that until yesterday he and Simon had always been together, had always done everything together, but there certainly hadn't been any "apron strings." He'd never thought of Simon as his "slave boy," either.

Outside, the sound of band music in the distance caught Edward's ear and drew him through the streets to the park where he'd watched the militia parade on national holidays before the war began. His eyes widened when he saw a motley group of elderly men and boys his brother's age—the home guard. It was easy to spot Duncan among them. He was almost a head taller than anyone else.

Hating the smug look on his brother's face, Edward watched the men go through the stylized drill until he was startled by a voice at his elbow.

"That new feller—is he your brother?"

Edward nodded. He didn't want to be rude, but he didn't particularly want to talk to the unkempt boy beside him.

"You two don't look much alike, 'cept for that dark hair you both got," the boy said, squinting at him. When Edward didn't answer, the boy added, "My brother's the one in the front row, the one with yaller hair. He ain't havin' near as good a time as yours is, though."

At that, Edward grinned in spite of himself, and the other boy said, "My name's Michael. Let's find something else to do."

For a moment, Edward held back, but then he said, "I'm Edward. Want to go explore those earthworks?"

"Sure," Michael said, adding, "That's where the real soldiers are at. Your pa in the war?"

"He's with General Lee's cavalry. What about yours?"

Michael kicked a stone out of his way and said, "Killed at Gettysburg. He was infantry. Cannon fodder's all them foot soldiers were." He looked appraisingly at Edward and said, "If your pa's cavalry, you must be rich."

"Not anymore," Edward said. "We're staying with my aunt because the Yankees took over our place on City Point."

Michael's eyes widened and he repeated, "City Point! Then you must of seen all them Yankee boats sailin' up the James."

By the time Edward had answered Michael's eager questions about the Yankees and about how his family had fled the plantation, the boys had almost reached the earthworks. Edward could see the trenches, with earth piled high to form a barrier in front of them. "How close will the soldiers let us come?" he asked.

"Most likely they're so tired of doin' nothin' they'll show us all around. Come on." Michael began to run, and Edward followed.

"Company's coming, men," one of the soldiers called as they approached. "You want the grand tour, lads?" he asked, and without waiting for an answer, he made a sweeping motion with his arm and announced, "These are the trenches, and that there's our bombproof. Go on in, if you want."

Edward looked with interest at the low entryway that seemed to lead right into the earthen bank. He ducked through it ahead of Michael and glanced around the small cavelike room. Disappointed, he saw that the bombproof was nothing but a hole in the ground with low log walls and a log roof built above it and then a thick layer of earth piled on top of it all.

The boys crawled out of the bombproof, and their self-appointed guide said, "Climb up on our firing step so you can see why the Yankees won't be coming into Petersburg."

Obediently, they stepped onto the earthen ledge, but neither boy was tall enough to see through the sandbag-protected openings where the sharpshooters would aim their rifles. "Here, I'll give you a boost," the soldier said, helping first Edward and then Michael to scramble onto the parapet.

Edward caught his breath at the sight of the line of earthworks that snaked along in both directions, as far as he could see. Forts here and there made him think of an angular snake swollen with square eggs it had swallowed. "What are all those small ditches out in front?" Edward asked, pointing.

"They're for our riflemen," the soldier answered, "in case a Yankee or two manages to make it across that open field."

For the first time, Edward realized the significance of the wide, cleared area that lay in front of the earthworks. It must be half a mile to that woods across the way, he thought, and any army trying to cross that space would be destroyed by the defenders. It would be suicide for the Yankees to attack Petersburg, he thought with relief.

"Thanks for showing us around," Edward said, jumping down from the parapet. "You coming, Michael?" he asked as he waited for the other boy to dust himself off.

On their way back to town, Michael said, "Want to race to that big ol' tree over there? Ready, set, go!"

Edward felt the dust splash around his feet as he ran, and soon he pulled ahead. He was going to win! He tagged the rough bark of the tree, and as he slowed to a stop he clasped his hands high above his head.

"What's that all about?" Michael asked as he caught up, panting.

Edward shrugged and turned away, embarrassed that in his elation he'd automatically responded with the victory signal he and Simon had shared. "I—I'm not used to winning," he said, adding silently, Not fair and square, anyway.

"Then you must not of raced anybody but that long-legged brother of yours. Hey, if you want, tomorrow me and you can go out to one of them forts and look around."

"Let's do that—you can stop by my aunt's house in the morning," Edward said, glad to change the subject. "Come on, and I'll show you where she lives."

When they reached Aunt Charlotte's, Michael looked from the wrought-iron fence around the yard to the towering trees and then at the wide, pillared porch across the front of the stately brick house. "Thought you said you wasn't rich," he challenged.

"We're not. We're poor relations," Edward said, glad Duncan couldn't hear him say that.

Michael gave a nod, apparently satisfied. "I'll come by right after breakfast," he said.

It was hard to imagine somebody not being sure he wanted to be your friend if you were rich, Edward thought as he climbed the steps to the porch. He was surprised at how glad he was that Michael *did* want to be his friend. Suddenly he stopped short. What if all those years he'd thought of Simon as his friend the other boy had thought of him as just another chore?

EARLY JUNE, 1864

Edward bent over his sketch pad, working unsuccessfully on a drawing. He'd erased so many times the page was worn thin, but he didn't dare start over. With paper so scarce that the *Petersburg Express* had shrunk to a single sheet, Edward knew he had to make his small supply of paper last.

Looking critically at his drawing, he decided it wasn't a bad picture—it just wasn't Simon. It was a broad-shouldered boy Simon's size, but you couldn't see his endless energy. You couldn't tell that he was full of ideas for things to do, or that he could do almost anything.

Edward thought of all the lean-to shelters the two of them had made in the woods when they were younger and of the elaborate precautions they had taken to avoid being followed to those lairs. They'd even devised a language of their own, with hand signs and gestures, so Duncan wouldn't overhear their plans and try to spoil them.

And then last summer, he and Simon had built a raft. They'd poled it up the creek and floated down again more times than they could count. And before the Yankees came, the two of them had been working on a canoe, hollowing out a log by burning and scraping it the same way Indians did long ago—except, of course, he and Simon used metal tools instead of stone ones. But now they'd never finish their canoe and learn to paddle it, never prove to Duncan that all their work hadn't been a waste of time.

Sighing, Edward reached for his pencil and titled the drawing *A Plantation Servant.* If he could draw Simon, then maybe he'd be able to stop thinking about him. "The least he could have done was say good-bye," he muttered. "I couldn't very well have made him come with us if he didn't want to." But I guess I would have tried to make him change his mind, Edward admitted silently.

For a moment, he thought he heard the rumble of thunder, but the day was clear and sunny. Edward listened, frowning, until he heard it again—now an almost continuous growl in the distance—and it dawned on him that it was artillery fire. Maybe Petersburg was being attacked. Maybe the Yankees who took over Riverview had marched down the road from City Point and were aiming all their cannon at the city's defenses.

Now the pounding of his heart drowned out all other sounds, and Edward had to force himself to think logically. The fighting was a long way from the city, he told himself. Petersburg was safe. But what about Father?

If he closed his eyes, Edward could picture Father, his saber drawn, galloping toward the enemy, could see the Yankee riflemen aim at the daring Confederate who led his men toward their position at breakneck speed. Edward's eyes flew open. He didn't want to see how that charge ended.

He left his sketch pad on the sitting room chair and started for the door, almost colliding with Jocasta and her feather duster. The servant's muttered words followed him: "Some folks' chillun musta been borned in a barn." Edward felt his face burn. He'd never minded when Elberta corrected him—she'd raised him, after all—but Jocasta was just plain mean.

His hands in his pockets, Edward headed toward the Confederate headquarters, where the casualty lists were posted. Whenever his concern for Father began to prey on his mind, Edward went to read through the lists of dead and wounded, hoping he wouldn't find Father's name—and hoping he wouldn't run into Duncan. Anytime Duncan wasn't drilling with the home guard, he was at the army telegrapher's office, waiting to hear news from the battlefronts as soon as it came in.

The war hadn't seemed so close at Riverview, Edward thought, in spite of the Yankee ships on the river and the prisoner exchanges that took place at the steamboat landing. But in Petersburg, with the streets full of soldiers and the line of earthworks snaking along the low hills surrounding the city, it was impossible to forget the war for long. The distant grumbling of artillery made Edward think of Father again, and he felt a dull ache somewhere deep inside.

By the time he got to the headquarters building, several people were clustered around the list outside the door. Apprehension twisted his stomach as he waited for an old man to read slowly down the list, his lips shaping each name. At last he left, and Edward took his place between a young girl and a stout woman already dressed in black mourning clothes.

His heart beat faster and faster as he neared the bottom of the list, and relief washed over him when he reached the end without finding his father's name. He turned away, spent with emotion, and almost bumped into Duncan.

"Are you reading those lists *again?*" his brother asked. "Father is quite able to look out for himself, you know."

Resentfully, Edward watched his brother go into the building. The war was nothing but a game to Duncan, he thought. A giant chess game with the Union and Confederate presidents as the two kings and their armies as all the other pieces. But the war was different. You couldn't set up your men again after a battle and have another go at it with everything just like it was before.

The trouble with Duncan, Edward thought as he started home, was that he had no imagination. He didn't see his pawns as infantrymen, didn't imagine his knights as cavalry and one of them as Father.

"Stop it," Edward commanded himself. The trouble with *him* was, he had too much imagination. Simon had known that, even though he'd said it a different way: It ain't the war that scares you, Marse Edward, you scare yourself, conjurin' up all sorts of things that ain't gonna happen.

So far, at least, none of the things he'd "conjured up" had happened, Edward thought as he neared Aunt Charlotte's house. Shells fired at Riverview by the Yankee gunboats hadn't exploded in his room at night when he was sleeping, bands of deserters hadn't swooped down on the plantation to take whatever they pleased, and the Negro soldiers who landed at City Point hadn't massacred the family.

Back at his aunt's house, Edward noticed that his sketch pad was gone. Sure that Jocasta had looked at his drawings when she took the pad to his room, he scowled. Then he turned and saw his sister standing in the doorway.

"I wish Elberta was here," Becky said. Her eyes looked large and dark in her small face.

"You know Elberta works at one of the cotton factories now, helping make shirts for our soldiers and tents for them to sleep in."

Becky nodded. "I know, but I still wish she was here."

"So do I," Edward admitted. He wished Aunt Charlotte would send her surly free Negro servant away and let Elberta take her place. That would serve Jocasta right.

JUNE 9, 1864

Edward looked up from his breakfast and frowned. Why was a church bell ringing on a Thursday?

"That's the courthouse bell," Mary Beth said, her hazel eyes wide.

Duncan jumped up from the table so quickly he knocked over his chair, and he ran out the door without a word. In the shocked silence that followed, Jocasta set the chair upright, and Edward noticed that she didn't mutter anything about "some folks' chillun." He thought she looked worried.

"Everybody's running into the street," Becky announced from the window.

Aunt Charlotte stood up and said, "Get your bonnets, girls."

Outside, Becky put her hands over her ears, and Edward was tempted to do the same. The relentless tolling of bells seemed to surround him, for now the church bells and firehouse bells had joined in. He gritted his teeth and tried to quiet the sense of dread that was building in him.

Neighbors gathered in little groups to speculate on what it all meant, and every time Edward heard the word "Yankees," his alarm grew. He tried to reassure himself with the thought that the battle he'd heard raging in the distance the week before had ended in another Confederate victory.

A commotion near the corner attracted Edward's attention, and he saw Duncan running toward them. "Yankees!" his brother shouted. "Cavalry heading this way, and no soldiers in the city! Anybody who can fire a gun, meet at the Rives farm."

"We never should have come here!" Mother cried, wringing her hands.

Breathing hard, Duncan stopped in front of her and said, "Don't worry. The home guard will protect the city until our soldiers can get here." He turned to leave, and his gaze fell on Edward. "I guess you'll have to be the man of the house while I'm away," he said dubiously, and then he was gone.

Edward pretended not to hear Jocasta mutter, "I'se more a man 'n he is," but he had to admit that she'd be more likely to frighten off a Yankee.

The little groups of neighbors scattered at the sound of shouts and hoofbeats, and several of the town's older citizens rode by, headed toward the earthworks. Edward felt a tug at his sleeve and looked down into Becky's worried face. "Why is Mama crying?" she asked. "And where did Duncan run off to?"

Ignoring his sister's first question, Edward said, "The home guard is going to drive the Yankee cavalry away from Petersburg, and Duncan's going to help." The little girl nodded, apparently satisfied, and Edward wished he could be reassured as easily. How long could a hundred or so old men and boys like Duncan hold off the enemy?

All around him, clumps of anxious women stood talking.

Edward saw Aunt Charlotte put a comforting arm around his weeping mother, and beside him, Mary Beth drew Becky closer to her. He felt alone, half glad that no one knew how scared he was and half wishing someone would try to make *him* feel better.

Think about something else, he told himself. He shut his eyes and concentrated on the fragrance of the magnolia blossoms and the warmth of the June sun. He listened to a mockingbird singing away just as though it were an ordinary morning.

"How come you're standin' there with your eyes shut?"

Michael. Edward's eyes popped open, and his friend asked, "Want to see what happens? I know a place we can watch from."

Before Edward could reply, Mary Beth said, "Better go while you have the chance, 'cause there may never be another battle this close to the city."

"Come on," Michael urged. "We don't want to miss nothin'."

"Where exactly are we going?" Edward asked, stalling.

"There's a ol' cowshed we can climb up on, oh, maybe half a mile back from the line," Michael said. "You comin'?"

Edward nodded and fell into step beside him. If Duncan and the other boys were brave enough to face the Yankee cavalry, *he* could certainly watch from a safe distance.

"What I'm hopin' is that we can pick 'em off as they ride between them two big banks of earth," Michael said.

It might work, Edward thought. His tutor had told him how in ancient times a small band of Spartans defended a narrow mountain pass against Persian invaders. The Spartans had fought to the last man in defense of their city.

Fought to the last man! Would the home guard do that? If they were all like Duncan, they would, but that still wouldn't keep the enemy cavalry from riding into Petersburg. Edward could almost see blue-clad horsemen filling the streets, their sabers flashing, could almost hear his mother's gasp as Yankee soldiers burst into the house.

Michael's voice was a welcome interruption. "Over there's the shed I told you 'bout. Come on."

Edward followed him across the scrubby pasture, and by the time he'd boosted Michael onto the sloping roof and struggled up himself he was surprised at how eager he was to see what would happen. He stretched out on his stomach and swept his eyes along the line of the earthworks until he saw the gap where the road breached the fortifications. It didn't look half a mile away to him. "Look," he cried, "they've hauled a wagon out to barricade the road!"

"They've piled up the rails from the farmer's fence, too," Michael said excitedly. "An' just in time, 'cause here come the Yankees!" He pointed to a cloud of dust that stretched along the horizon and moved steadily toward them.

Behind the barricade, tiny figures took their places—figures Edward knew were men. Men, and boys like Michael's older brother and Duncan. Suddenly, Edward was aware of the dull thud of hoofbeats, and then the forms of mounted soldiers emerged from the reddish haze. His breath burst from his lungs in a hoarse cry when the little group of defenders began to fire and a cavalryman fell from his saddle.

Flattening himself against the shed roof, Edward lay with his eyes squeezed shut, catching only occasional words of Michael's excited commentary. But a change in his tone focused Edward's attention when Michael cried, "They've dismounted! Them Yankees are tryin' to surround our men!"

Edward lifted his head and saw the home guard retreating, carrying their dead and injured. *What if one of them was Duncan?*

"Come on!" Michael cried, scuttling down to the edge of the roof and dropping to the ground.

Edward followed, his heart beating wildly. As the boys ran toward home, the back of Edward's neck prickled at the thought of thousands of Yankees streaming into the city.

Sweating and breathless, the boys stopped to rest in the shade of a tree. "Listen," Michael said. "What's that?"

At first Edward thought he was hearing the thumping of his own heart, but as the sound grew louder he knew it was hoofbeats—horsemen coming from the city! He felt totally disoriented until in a blur of gray, Confederate cavalrymen thundered past on their way to meet the enemy.

Michael stood looking after them, but Edward said, "Come on! We don't want to be here if the Yankees drive 'em back!" Michael streaked away, and it was all Edward could do to keep up with him.

Inside the city again, the boys heard shouts and moments later they saw horses charging toward them, pulling cannon through crowds of cheering citizens. "That should take care of those Yankees," Edward said when the artillery had passed. But Michael didn't answer. He had run along behind the artillerymen and now stood halfway up the block, staring after them.

Suddenly Edward realized someone was calling him. "Oh, Edward, I was afraid something had happened to you!" It was Mary Beth, and before he knew what was happening, she was hugging him—right there on the street! As he struggled out of her grasp, she said, "Now tell me all about it."

Backing away from his cousin, Edward saw that her eyes were feverishly bright. Little tendrils of chestnut hair had escaped from her bonnet and framed her flushed, eager-looking face. Why, he wondered, would Mary Beth want to hear about the battle when all he wanted was to be as far away from it as possible? And what would his cousin think of him if she knew he'd run away?

Avoiding her eyes, Edward said, "You'd better wait and get a firsthand description from Duncan when he gets back." *If* he gets back. The words "fought to the last man" echoed in Edward's mind.

Mary Beth's hands flew to her face and she said, "How could I be so thoughtless? Of course you don't want to talk about the battle when you're worried sick about your brother! Can you ever forgive me?"

"There's nothing to forgive, Mary Beth. I'd just rather not talk about it." He didn't even want to think about it—about the terror that had gripped him when he saw the billowing cloud of dust that rose as the Yankees approached, about the horror he'd felt when the first cavalryman was shot from his horse.

Edward looked at the groups of anxious women waiting for news of the sons and husbands who had rushed to defend the city. Some of them flinched at the sound of artillery fire or the sputtering of rifles in the distance, afraid for someone they loved, but they didn't seem to be afraid for themselves. Were they really that brave, or were they hiding their fear, as he was?

At least Michael had been scared, too, Edward thought. He could hardly believe how fast the other boy had run.

Less than ten miles away, Simon leaned against a tree and watched the Negro troops drill. He noticed that the brass buttons and belt plates on their uniforms gleamed as brightly as the ones he'd polished for his lieutenant the night before. And he saw that the men went through the drill procedure flawlessly, performing each step with precision as their white officer shouted commands. If only Edward were here to see what Negroes could do when they were given a chance.

He'd done it, Simon realized with satisfaction. He'd finally trained himself not to think of Edward as *Marse* Edward. "Marse" was the only Negro dialect Simon had used at the Great House, and he'd told himself it meant "young mister" instead of "master." After all, Edward never ordered him around the way Marse Duncan—the way *Duncan* had Ambrose.

Edward had been more like a friend than a master, Simon thought. They'd looked after each other. He'd taught Edward how to swim and throw, and Edward had taught him how to read and write. He'd helped Edward stand up for himself against his brother, and Edward had stood up for him more than once against Miss Emily.

"I never knew how lonely freedom was gonna be," Simon muttered. He thought of the last time he'd seen Edward—the day the soldiers landed at City Point and turned the plantation into a Union camp. The day *he* became free.

Thinking about being free still made Simon tingle with excitement, even though his life hadn't changed much. When he was Edward's slave, the family had called him a servant, but now that he was the Lieutenant's servant, the officers called him a "darky," or "one of our contrabands."

Contrabands. Simon thought of the first time he'd heard that word, the day the lieutenant had told him, "You can go ahead and cook your own rations, but I'll be eating over at the house from now on. One of our contrabands has set herself up in the summer kitchen to cook for the officers."

"What's contrabands, sir?" he had asked.

"*You're* contraband. You and all the other slaves that ran off from their masters and follow the Union army now."

"'Contraband' means free Negroes?" he had asked hopefully.

The lieutenant gave him a scornful look. "It means Negro refugees. President Lincoln may have *said* you people were free," the lieutenant went on, "but it's this army that will *make* you free—if we ever win this blessed war. You people wouldn't have a chance if we didn't look after you."

As Simon remembered that conversation, he felt the same surge of resentment that had swept over him when he'd watched the lieutenant stride confidently toward the Great House. Shifting his attention back to the Negro soldiers on the drill field, Simon felt a stir of envy. They were part of the Union army, not contrabands who followed after it, depending on the army for food and protection.

"Looks to me like the army depends on the contrabands 'most as much as the other way 'round," Simon muttered, thinking of how Serena, the plantation cook, had gone from preparing meals for the family to preparing meals for the officers. Other slaves worked as washerwomen for them, and a couple of the field hands looked after the officers' horses. He was working for his keep, too, Simon reminded himself. He was looking after the lieutenant the way he used to look after Edward.

How was Edward managing without him? Simon knew the white boy missed him. You couldn't spend almost your whole life with someone and not miss him when he was gone. But more than that, Edward needed him. Depended on him. And not just for what he did for him, either. "I was more of a brother to that boy than Marse Duncan ever was," Simon whispered.

He thought of his own brother, Ambrose, and sighed. Ambrose had been the best brother a boy could have. If Marse Duncan—If *Duncan* had been like Edward instead of so high and mighty, Ambrose never would have left Riverview and run off with the field hands two years ago.

Everybody he'd ever cared about was gone now, Simon thought. First Ambrose left, and then last summer their ma had died of a fever in spite of everything Miss Emily and the doctor could do. Even his pa was gone from one of the plantations across the river, sold to pay off his owner's debts. And a month ago Edward had left for Petersburg, and *he* had stayed behind.

It didn't pay to care about anybody, Simon decided, because sooner or later, one way or another, whether they meant to or not, they'd up and leave you. At least Edward hadn't wanted to leave him, Simon thought, remembering how the white boy had called his name over and over again.

Simon turned his attention back to the soldiers, trying now to memorize the sequence of movements they made as they drilled with their rifles. "Next time, I'm bringin' those field glasses so's I can see just what it is they do," he muttered.

The field glasses made him think of Edward again, and Simon remembered how the white boy had grabbed the rope and slid to the ground, leaving the field glasses on the tree platform. And then *he* had left them there, planning to return and watch the Negro soldiers. He'd never meant to keep the glasses for good, but after Edward left, Simon realized that they were his now, and he'd slipped away from the lieutenant to retrieve them.

Tired of watching the soldiers drill, Simon made his way to the lieutenant's tent. It was hard to believe that a month ago this had been Miss Emily's lawn, he thought as he walked through the camp. He'd never forget the way thousands of Negro soldiers had swarmed over the plantation and turned it into a city of tents.

Simon squatted down to light the fire he had laid earlier so he could heat water for the lieutenant to wash with before he went to the Great House for the evening meal. "Never knew nobody that had to be half so clean," he muttered. He blew on the tiny curl of flame, then leaned back to watch it spread. The familiar ritual reminded him of all the fires he'd kindled in Edward's room, one each morning from early fall through April for as long as he could remember. He wondered who would do that for Edward when cold weather came again. . . .

That night, Simon moved his pallet from inside the lieutenant's tent to the area sheltered by the tent's canvas fly, hoping he might catch a breeze. He didn't see how anyone could sleep in the sweltering heat.

The lieutenant wasn't even trying to. With his boxlike traveling desk on his lap, he sat writing in his journal. Now and then he swatted at the cloud of insects that hovered around his candle, or brushed away a moth that landed on his paper. Simon watched him, wondering how he could find something to write about each evening when every day was exactly like the one before. Roll calls. Inspections. Drills. . . .

The next morning, Simon woke before the camp was stirring. From the pale light he judged it was a good half hour before reveille, but with the lieutenant snoring away on his cot there wasn't much chance of falling asleep again.

Simon stood up, and his eyes fell on the journal lying open on the traveling desk where the officer had left it. The man's snores came from the tent with comforting regularity as Simon picked up the book and began to read.

The bulk of our army still faces Lee's not many miles from here at a place called Cold Harbor where we suffered terrible losses. It's not for nothing the newspapers call our general "Butcher Grant."

Here in camp, all is calm but unbearably hot. My little darky continues to take the best care of me, heating water so I may wash and shave, polishing my leather and shining my brass, running my errands, and tidying things around our camp. He stands behind my chair in the plantation house at mealtime now, anticipating my every need and keeping the cursed flies away.

The boy seems quite content. Perhaps the Rebs are telling the truth when they say these people are satisfied with their lot and need to be looked after. Certainly this boy needs me to provide his daily bread and the canvas roof over his head.

There was more, but Simon didn't bother to read it. He wanted to rip out the page, but he controlled his rush of anger and put the book back exactly as he'd found it. Without making a sound, he took the tin plate and cup the lieutenant had given him and rolled them up in his blanket, along with the field glasses Edward had left behind.

As Simon slung the blanket roll over his shoulder, he saw his fork and spoon and slipped them in his pocket. The lieutenant was still snoring when Simon stepped out from under the tent fly onto the "street" between the officers' wall tents.

When reveille sounded, Simon was walking between rows of inverted Vs—shelter tents where the ordinary soldiers slept. He wondered how long it would take the lieutenant to figure out that his "darky" was gone for good and not simply getting water for him to wash with. "I don't need him," Simon muttered. "I can look after myself."

Soldiers moved sleepily about the camp now, but none of them showed any interest in Simon. He walked until he smelled salt pork frying and was conscious of his hunger. Following his nose, he soon found himself beyond the soldiers' camp, near where the supply wagons were parked. He stopped to stare at the rows of wagons with their rounded canvas tops.

"A gran' sight, ain't it?" someone said, and Simon turned to see a heavyset man with grizzled hair. His dark skin was lined, but his eyes were bright and curious. "You looks like you runnin' 'way, boy."

"I'se *goin'* 'way, but I ain't runnin'," Simon said, automatically slipping into dialect. His eyes moved to the slabs of pork the man was lifting from his skillet. Watching him add slices of potato to the grease in the pan, Simon felt the saliva begin to flow.

The man squinted up at him and asked, "You want breakfas'? Won't be long till dis ready."

Simon quickly unrolled his blanket and brought out his cup and plate. "I ain't never seen so many wagon before," he said, his eyes straying in their direction.

"Dey carry everything dis army need," the man said.

"You drive one, uncle?" Simon asked.

The man nodded. "Ol' Hap drive one of dem baggage wagon." He reached for Simon's plate and heaped it with pork and fried potatoes, then filled his tin cup with coffee. By the end of the meal, Simon knew all about the old man—how he had hoed cotton in South Carolina for more years than he could count, and how he had worked for the army for the past year. But Simon was careful to steer the conversation away from himself. He knew that field hands didn't always take kindly to house servants.

"I could use a boy to help 'round camp, if you ain't goin' nowheres in partic'lar," Uncle Hap said, sipping his coffee.

"What you want me to do?"

"Look after de mule team," Uncle Hap replied, "an' help wi' de cookin'." When a man crawled out of one of the other tents that faced the wagon park, Uncle Hap said, "You start peelin' taters, an' I'll slice off some mo' meat."

Simon reached for his knife. He'd rather work for Uncle Hap and the other teamsters than be some white officer's darky.

JUNE 14 AND 15, 1864

Simon took a step and sank into river muck above his ankles, pulled his other foot free and splashed forward. The string of mules he was taking for water followed him eagerly, and he grinned at the obscene sucking noise that accompanied each raised hoof.

At the water's edge, the mud had been churned into an almost liquid ooze that fanned out into the water as the mules moved through it. Simon felt sorry for the beasts—and a little sorry for himself, too. This was nothing like his dreams of freedom. He was doing more work, and certainly dirtier work, than he'd done when he was a slave. "At least nobody's makin' me do this," Simon muttered. "I'm doin' it of my own free will."

One of the mules flicked his ear toward the sound of Simon's voice. "That's right, ol' mule," the boy said, "I got free will."

Looking after Edward hadn't seemed like work at all, he thought as he led the mules back to the corral, and looking after the lieutenant had been an easy job. Still, he'd rather look after mules than that lieutenant, Simon decided, remembering what the man had written in his journal.

Later, Simon was walking through the camp when he saw a long line of soldiers waiting in front of the commissary. A group of men headed back toward the campsites with bulging haversacks slung over their shoulders, and Simon caught the words "three days' rations." Why would the men be given three days' meals at once, unless—? He turned and raced along the packed-earth company streets, headed for the wagon park.

"You hear de news?" Uncle Hap called as Simon ran into the teamsters' camp. "Army got it marchin' order. Yessir," he said, draining his tin cup, "our boys gonna have a chance to show what dey made of. To make up for bein' left behin' when de army went to Col' Harbor."

From what Simon knew about the battle at Cold Harbor, he figured that the Negro soldiers were lucky they'd been left behind, but he kept his thoughts to himself. "I figger dey was fixin' to leave dis place," he said.

"You can come wi' de wagon train if you want," Uncle Hap offered.

Simon's spirits soared at the thought of actually following the Negro troops to this new battle, but all he said was, "Dat wagon ain't got no seat, Uncle Hap. Where we gonna ride?"

"Driver, he ride on de mule closest to de wagon, on de left. You can walk alongside."

Simon nodded. He could do that. He'd be marching, just like the soldiers.

That evening, Simon lay on his blanket, his body exhausted but his mind still alert. He could hear mules stamping and whuffing all along the wagon train, could hear Uncle Hap's regular breathing. It sounded like "T'mor—row . . . T'mor—row . . ."

Tomorrow he would leave City Point and march with the Union army! It wasn't the same as being a soldier, of course, but it promised to be the most exciting thing that had ever happened to him.

It was still pitch black when Simon woke the next morning to the staccato blare of a bugle. Dazed with sleep, he helped Uncle Hap fill the mules' feedbox with oats. He was beginning to wonder why they'd all been awakened so early if nothing was going to happen when another bugle call sounded, a cadence that was new to Simon. Then, through the darkness came the sound of horses' hooves, followed by a third bugle call and a sound he couldn't quite place.

As the sound grew louder Simon knew it was the tramp of feet and the clank of canteens—the sound of an army on the move. It seemed to go on forever. Finally, Uncle Hap's voice came through the lifting darkness. "Won't be long now."

Far ahead of them, Simon heard shouts and then the creaking of wheels, but it was almost daylight by the time the wagon in front of theirs finally began to roll. When Uncle Hap climbed onto one of the mules and cracked his long black whip above the animals' backs, Simon fell into step beside the old man.

"Yessir," Uncle Hap said above the creaking of the

wagon, "from what I hear tell, dis army gonna take Petersburg today."

Petersburg? That was where Edward had gone! "I—I thought it Richmond dey want. Ain't Richmond de Reb cap'tal?" Simon asked, hoping the old man was wrong.

But Uncle Hap shook his head and said, "Dey done try an' try to take Richmond an' ain't had no luck at all. I hear dey figure on takin' Petersburg 'nstead, 'cause all de South's railroads come through dere."

Simon didn't see what railroads had to do with it until Uncle Hap added, "If dey can stop dem train from bringin' ol' Lee an' his army food an' what all, dem Rebel can't fight no more."

"Somebody I know live dere in Petersburg. What you reckon gonna happen to him?" Simon asked tentatively.

"He gonna be free, jus' like we is," the old man said.

"But what gonna happen to all dem white folk?"

Uncle Hap laughed. "Dey gonna be *scared*. But soldier, dey don' hurt no women an' chillun. Or ol' folk. Dey steal a li'l, wreck a li'l, but dey don' hurt nobody."

The wagon train slowed to a stop, and as the dust began to settle Uncle Hap grumbled, "Seem like all we do is sit in de sun an' wait." Simon didn't like waiting in the blazing sun either, but in spite of Uncle Hap's reassurances, he was less eager for the army to continue its march now that he knew where it was headed.

They hadn't been on their way long before Simon heard shots, and then a burst of artillery fire rent the air. "Would you look at dat!" Uncle Hap exclaimed, and hearing the excitement in the old man's voice, Simon climbed up onto the wagon's toolbox for a better view. He raised his field glasses and saw soldiers running toward the Rebel cannon that had fired. "Dey's our boys, Simon," the old man said excitedly. "Our boys!"

Sure enough, Negro troops swarmed up the hill. Simon gasped when the Rebels fired again and men staggered and fell to the ground. He didn't want to watch, but he couldn't tear his eyes away from the Negro soldiers who surged forward only to be forced back again. Soon the ground was strewn with dead and wounded men, but still Simon watched.

More Negro soldiers joined the battle and pressed forward. At last the enemy shelling stopped, and Simon held his breath. The Rebels were hauling away one of their huge guns, lashing their horses frantically, but— Yes! The other gun was captured. Simon laughed aloud as he watched the black troops clap each other on the shoulders and dance joyfully around it. Serious again when he saw stretcher bearers moving among the wounded, Simon lowered the field glasses and asked, "How many men you figger was kill in dat battle?"

"Heck, dat weren't no battle, boy," Uncle Hap said scornfully. "Dat weren't hardly a skirmish."

Suddenly Simon's mouth felt dry. He scooped up a few handfuls of water from the bucket hanging at the back of the wagon before he sat down in the shade of the white-topped vehicle. If what he'd just seen was only a skirmish, he didn't want to watch a battle.

The sun was high in the sky by the time the wagon train was under way once more, but after another dusty mile it stopped again. This time, at least, they were in the woods and not waiting in the blazing sun, Simon thought. But as he swatted at the gnats that hovered around his face, he began to wish for something—anything!—to happen. After what seemed like hours, Uncle Hap said, "Stretch dem leg a bit an' find out what goin' on up dere."

Simon figured he'd walked close to half a mile before he could see the beginning of the wagon train ahead of him and beyond that, soldiers lounging in the shade. Some of them had kindled small fires to boil water for coffee, but others seemed to be napping. How many of them there were!

Suddenly, Simon stopped short. He thought he'd heard someone call his name, but that was impossible. Then he heard a familiar whistle, and his heart leaped. Looking back, he saw a lanky dark-skinned soldier striding toward him. It couldn't be Ambrose, he told himself, because when his brother left Riverview he'd warned that they were saying good-bye forever.

But it *was* Ambrose—and how grand he looked in his uniform! With a cry, Simon ran and hurled himself at the older youth. He felt himself crushed against the roughness of his brother's jacket for a moment before Ambrose held him at arm's length. Concern on his face, the young soldier ignored Simon's excited flood of questions and demanded, "What you doin' here? Didn't I tell you to stay on dat plantation where you was look after?"

Simon quickly told Ambrose how the family had fled when the Union army took over Riverview. "Marse Duncan would like to die if he seen you wearin' dat uniform," he added.

"He ain't my master no more," Ambrose retorted, "an' you still ain't tol' me what you doin' here."

Simon knew Ambrose's sternness masked his worry. "I'se wid one of dem teamster, an' he done sent me to find out why we stop," he explained.

"Dis be why," Ambrose said grimly. He motioned for Simon to follow him.

At the edge of the woods, Simon stopped and stared. Slowly he shifted the strap of his field glasses so they hung around his neck instead of across his chest, and he lifted the glasses to his eyes. As the scene before him rushed closer, he almost fell backward.

Beyond the woods Simon saw a level clearing perhaps half a mile wide, and then a line of Rebel earthworks, its contour broken by square forts that angled forward. He caught his breath at the sight of the gleaming barrels of Rebel cannon, then let his gaze linger on a wide ditch in front of the earthworks. Just like the moat around the castle in Edward's book, he thought.

Moving the glasses a little, Simon saw what seemed to be sharpened poles rising diagonally toward him on the near side of the ditch to form a barrier, and beyond those, a series of smaller ditches. "What are de hole in front of dem sharp thing?"

"Pit fer de riflemen. Now you see why we's stop?"

Nodding, Simon offered the field glasses to his brother, but Ambrose shook his head and said, "I'se gonna see it close up."

"Dere still gonna be a battle?" Simon didn't see how anyone could cross that open area to storm the earthworks.

Ambrose gave a humorless laugh. "You think dat stop dem general? But don' you worry none," he added quickly. "Artillery gonna cover us while we cross dat field. Dem Reb won't be able to fire at us for fear of havin' dere own head blowed off."

The ground before Simon blurred as he followed Ambrose back through the woods. No wonder Uncle Hap had said the fighting this morning was hardly a skirmish. Simon stumbled along, hardly aware of where he was, until he heard Ambrose greet his friends and say, "Dis here my brother, Simon. He gonna camp wid us." Then, one at a time, Ambrose pointed to the men, saying their names: Luke, Sam, Homer.

Simon nodded to acknowledge each introduction, but he didn't even try to remember the names. He thought of the wide expanse of open land the men must cross and half wished Ambrose hadn't spotted him. Then he could have gone on believing that his brother had safely reached the North instead of knowing he'd been—

"Dey say we gonna 'tack in less 'n a hour," one young soldier told Ambrose, his voice shaking.

Simon knew he couldn't face spending that last hour with Ambrose. "I gotta go now. Uncle Hap say for me to bring back news." He took a deep breath and managed to choke out, "G-good luck in de battle."

Without waiting for a response he started back along the road, but Ambrose called after him, "Find yo'self a place so's you can watch it wi' dem field glass."

When Simon reached the wagon, Hap and the other teamsters stopped their card game to listen intently as he told them what he'd learned. After he finished, there was silence until Hap declared, "Now *dat* gonna be a *battle.*"

The minutes seemed to crawl by. Simon leaned against a tree and brooded about Ambrose until finally one of the teamsters said, "It long pas' a hour. Maybe dere ain't gonna be no battle." But before anyone could reply, a blast of artillery fire told them the attack had begun.

At least this time it was Union cannon he was hearing, Simon thought. He hoped the continuous firing really would keep the Rebels from shooting as Ambrose and the others ran toward the earthworks. The weight of the field glasses hanging around his neck reminded Simon that his brother had told him to watch the battle, and he squared his shoulders. If Ambrose wanted him to watch, he would watch.

Uncle Hap and the other teamsters were intent on their game again, and since it seemed easier to simply leave instead of trying to explain about meeting Ambrose, Simon slipped away. The pounding artillery fire was almost deafening, but he pressed his hands over his ears and continued down the dusty road he had walked along earlier that day. Clouds of black smoke drifted back to him, and he coughed.

Not far from the road stood a dead pine, and Simon cut through the woods and headed for it. He made his way up the tree, limb to limb, scarcely noticing when small branches snapped off or scraped his skin and tore at his clothes. When he thought he'd climbed high enough to have a clear view, Simon wrapped one arm around the scaly trunk and looked toward the Rebel fortifications.

He gasped when he saw a wave of blue surging toward the earthworks, then raised the field glasses and saw that anonymous sea become a churning mass of men. Scanning the field, Simon searched for the Negro soldiers, and when he trained his glasses on the men in the lead, he saw that they were black. Hardly breathing, he watched them run full speed, straight toward the rifle pits where the Rebels lay firing at them.

Simon bit his lip as one after another, Negro soldiers fell. But the men behind them came on as relentlessly as the tide, and then— Then the Rebel riflemen turned and ran back toward their defenses! A cheer broke from Simon's throat. He watched the Negro soldiers zigzag through the tangle of sharpened branches in pursuit of their enemies . . . disappear briefly into the ditches . . . reappear as they scrambled up the sloping wall of the earthworks . . . and vanish on the other side.

"They've taken Petersburg," Simon said aloud, and then in hushed tones he corrected himself: "*We've* taken Petersburg!"

Inside the city, it took a moment for Edward to realize that the firing had stopped. The silence seemed unnatural after two hours of listening to the spitting of rifles and the jarring *BADOOM!* of artillery.

"Thank God the line held," Mary Beth said, her voice hushed.

But Duncan said flatly, "If the line had held, the Yankees would still be firing."

"Does that mean—" Mary Beth stopped in mid-sentence

when Aunt Charlotte cleared her throat and looked pointedly at Becky.

Duncan hesitated a moment and then said, "I doubt that the few men we had spread out along the line were able to turn them back."

Edward stared at his brother. If the Yankees hadn't been turned back, did that mean they were coming into Petersburg? Maybe even coming right into Aunt Charlotte's house? What would become of them all if some Yankee officer gave them an hour to leave here? Edward's racing thoughts were interrupted by Becky's voice.

"Maybe they've stopped shooting at each other 'cause it's dark out."

Duncan's expression softened when he looked at his little sister, and he said, "Don't worry, Becky. I'll go see what's happening."

"You'll do no such thing," Mother said. "I won't have you leaving the house when we have no idea what—"

"I'll be fine, Mother," Duncan interrupted. "You mustn't worry so."

Mother stared after Duncan as he strode from the room. Frowning as he watched his brother, Edward decided that after taking part in last week's battle Duncan must think he was a man. He did act more grown-up, Edward mused. Now that his brother had seen men killed—and had fired at the enemy himself—he finally seemed to realize what *he* had known all along: The war was a matter of life and death. But instead of being afraid, Duncan wanted more than ever to be a part of it, wanted to have a hand in beating the Yankees.

And now the Yankees had come to Petersburg. Edward's

chest felt so tight he could hardly breathe. Was he the only one who was scared? Glancing around the room, he saw that his mother's face was pale and her hands clutched her needlework, but he couldn't tell whether she was afraid or worried about Duncan.

Edward turned his attention to Aunt Charlotte. She was rocking vigorously, and her knitting needles clacked as she added row after row to the scarf she was making. Almost hypnotized by her movements, he watched as the scarf grew longer and longer, its length puddling on the floor at her feet. And still she rocked and knitted. *Aunt Charlotte was afraid, too!* Somehow, knowing that made Edward feel better.

Beside him, Becky asked, "Which do you want to do while we wait for Duncan to come back, play a game or listen to one of Mary Beth's stories?"

"Listen to a story," Edward said quickly, and he allowed himself to be lulled by his cousin's voice as she began a long and complicated fairy tale. It was nothing like the stories of magic and witchcraft that Simon had told at night when they were supposed to be asleep, Edward thought drowsily. Stories worth listening to . . .

Edward woke with a start to hear a man's voice. Uncle Gilbert had come home, and in the soft glow of the gaslight, Aunt Charlotte's plain face shone with love and pleasure. If his uncle was here, Edward realized, that meant reinforcements had been rushed to Petersburg from across the Appomattox River. They were safe!

"More than a mile of our defenses fell to the Yankees," his uncle was saying. "If they'd pushed on, they could have taken the city, but our men are pouring into Petersburg now. My unit arrived in time to help dig new trenches closer to town." Uncle Gilbert gave Edward a weary smile and said, "Well, look who woke up. Come see what one of the prisoners we took last week had on him."

Wide awake now, Edward crossed the room to stand by Uncle Gilbert's chair. "What do you think of this?" his uncle asked, bringing something out of his uniform pocket.

Edward reached for it. "A metal pencil?"

"Give it a twist and see what happens."

"More lead comes out!" Edward was delighted.

Uncle Gilbert smiled and said, "You can have it, if you think it would be useful in your artwork."

His artwork. Edward felt a flood of affection for his uncle. "Oh, thank you, sir!" he said.

His uncle waved away his thanks and turned to Mother. "I was glad to see Duncan pitching in to help our men dig a new defensive line," he said. "We're going to need all the manpower we can get, because if what I hear is true, all of Grant's Yankee army is on the way to Petersburg."

Mother leaned forward and asked, "What about General Lee's army? Is it on the way here, too?"

"I certainly hope so, Emily. We all hope so."

"If General Lee's army comes, maybe we'll see Father," Becky said eagerly. "Wouldn't that be wonderful, Edward?"

But Edward barely heard his sister's question. He'd just had a terrible thought: If the two great armies met at Petersburg, this evening's battle would seem like nothing at all.

Simon's head pounded even though the Union artillery had been still for some time now. He peered through the darkness, the pride he'd felt when the Negro soldiers stormed the Rebel earthworks overshadowed by uncertainty. Was Ambrose one of the men who had made it all the way to the Rebel works, or was his body lying somewhere on that open plain? Though the night was warm, Simon felt a chill. Maybe he should go back to Uncle Hap. But would the wagon still—

Flickers of light near the Rebel earthworks caught Simon's attention. Torches. Some of the men were coming back! It seemed to take forever, but at last they reached the woods. Simon searched the faces that gleamed in the torchlight, and relief swept over him when at last he saw his brother. "Ambrose!" he cried.

"What's wrong, 'Brose?" Simon asked when he had pushed his way through the milling crowd. He noticed now that the men seemed angry rather than triumphant.

"First dey didn't let us take dat city, an' den dey send us back here," Ambrose said, his eyes bright with fury. "Dem gen'ral send us back an' set white soldier to guard all de fort *we* took. Like dey didn't think we could hold 'em."

In an instant, the men were all talking at once, their voices agitated. "You mean you didn't take Petersburg?" Simon asked in disbelief.

Ambrose scowled. "Dem gen'ral gonna make us wait 'round till dat Rebel army git here 'nstead of lettin' us take dat city when de takin' good!"

There were murmurs of agreement, and someone added, "Gonna git us kilt stormin' dem work again. I reckon dat why dey brung us back—so's it black men an' not white gittin' kilt."

Simon's mind reeled as it struck him that Negroes who had been valuable property to their masters might be worth nothing at all to a northern general.

JUNE 21, 1864, AND THE FOLLOWING DAY

Simon sat on an overturned crate in front of the shelter tent he shared with Ambrose in his company's camp behind the lines. Simon liked living with Ambrose and his messmates, liked waking up beside his brother. He even liked it when Ambrose bossed him around the way he always used to.

" 'Don' do nothin' foolish just 'cause somebody dare you,' " Simon mimicked. "'You free now—stan' tall so everybody know it.'" He grinned, pleased that he sounded so much like his brother.

Simon glanced up when he heard excited voices, and he saw the men streaming into camp. What was going on? He dropped the stick he'd been whittling and went to the edge of the "street" that ran between the rows of tents. But the men's words made little sense until he heard the name "Father Abraham" and knew they were talking about the president.

Slowly, Simon began to piece it all together. The president had been touring the front line, and the men had met him on his way back to City Point. They had seen Abraham Lincoln and he had spoken to them! If only *he* could have seen him, too.

Simon saw Ambrose hurrying toward him, followed by

Luke, the only one of the messmates Simon didn't like. Ambrose's face glowed with excitement, and he called, "I touch him, Simon—I touch de man dat make us free!"

Quoting the young lieutenant, Simon said, "De pres'-dent *said* we was free, but it dis army gonna *make* us free."

"If dem general don' make so many mistake dey git us all kill first," Luke grumbled as he sank down onto one of the crates that served as seats.

Simon scowled, remembering how the army had missed its chance to take Petersburg, remembering how Ambrose's angry prophesy had come true. By the time the Union generals ordered an attack on the city, the Rebel army *had* arrived in Petersburg, and thousands of northern soldiers died before the order came to dig trenches of their own opposite the Rebel earthworks.

"Don' you pay Luke no 'tention," Ambrose said earnestly. "Dem general make mistake like anybody else, but dis army still de best thing ever happen to us. You stick wi' dis army, an' you be fine."

"I'se gonna stick wid *you,*" Simon said. Now that he'd found his brother again, nothing was going to separate them.

Edward moved his eyes across the pages of his book, but he had no idea what he was reading. It sounded like the Yankees were shelling the city again, and after each *BADOOM!* he held his breath and listened for the telltale whine that would mean a shell was coming close. Uncle Gilbert had said it wasn't likely that one would reach their neighborhood and that they shouldn't worry unless they heard a high-pitched whistling sound.

But yesterday a house a block away had been hit, and Mother had forbidden him and Becky to go outside. Edward scowled at the idea of being lumped with Becky in his mother's mind. It embarrassed him to be sitting uselessly inside, pretending to read, while Duncan helped dig trenches for the new Confederate position a mile outside of town and the women—

Beside him, a small voice said, "I want Mama," and Edward turned to see Becky's pale face.

"Now, Becky, you know Mother and Aunt Charlotte are helping at one of the hospitals."

"Then I want Mary Beth."

"She and her friend Agatha went to one of the churches to help roll bandages." When Edward saw his sister's lower lip begin to tremble, he quickly said, "I could play a game with you, if you'd like."

Her face lit up, and she said, "I'll get the dominoes."

While everyone else was doing something for the Confederate cause, he was playing nursemaid to his sister, Edward thought glumly as she emptied the dominoes onto the table.

After they'd played for half an hour, Becky said, "I'm not scared anymore, Edward. Will you always play with me so I won't be scared?"

Before he could reply, Jocasta came into the room and said, "Marse Edward, I need salt, an' I ain't got time to go to de store, so I'se wonderin' could you walk down dere for me jus' dis once."

Edward looked up, surprised. This was the first time his aunt's servant had spoken directly to him since they'd arrived. Before he could answer, Becky announced, "Mama said for Edward to stay inside today."

The woman glanced at her disdainfully and said, "I'd not be de one tellin' dat he done lef' de house."

Indignantly, the child said, "I'd never tell on Edward!"

"So, Marse Edward," Jocasta drawled, "is you goin', or is you scared?"

Edward felt a flare of anger. "I'm going," he said shortly. How dare Jocasta talk to him like that? He'd show her. He was going to be scared no matter where he was, so he might as well be outside. It was one thing for Mother to keep Becky in the house while the shelling was going on, but a boy his age?

"Have de cost put on Marse Gilbert's account," Jocasta called after him.

As Edward stepped onto the porch, a sudden *BADOOM! BADOOM! BADOOM!* of artillery fire made his pulse race, but he forced his legs to carry him down the steps and out the gate. If Jocasta was watching, she wouldn't see him flinch.

Edward started off toward Mr. Endicott's store, managing to walk at a normal pace even though his skin crawled. The little hairs on his arms stood on end as he imagined being blown to bits by a Yankee shell, and he reminded himself that the whistling sound would give him plenty of warning.

"Here behind General Lee's lines is the safest place to be," Edward whispered. That was what Uncle Gilbert had said. But if it was like this in Petersburg, Edward thought, giving a start at a new burst of artillery fire, what must it be like outside the city, where Father was?

Uncle Gilbert had explained that General Lee's cavalry had to protect the railroads that led into Petersburg, bringing food and other goods. "You mustn't be disappointed if you don't see much of your father even though he's close by now," he'd added, "because everything depends on keeping those trains running, and our cavalry's stretched thin."

Edward hadn't gone far when he heard the measured beating of drums and then the sound of a band playing. Just knowing that Confederate soldiers were nearby made him feel safer, and he stopped to watch a newly arrived regiment march from the railroad depot toward army headquarters. But to Edward's disappointment, the men weren't marching so much as simply walking along, and they were a thin and ragged-looking lot, too. When he raised his eyes to the men's sunburned faces, though, Edward felt better. They looked fearless. And determined.

The soldiers at the front of the group suddenly broke into cheers, and Edward turned to see women and young girls hurrying from their homes to line the street. Some of the girls waved small Confederate flags, and others tossed flowers or blew kisses. None of them seemed worried about enemy shells.

Edward set off again, alert now rather than afraid, and soon he came to Mr. Endicott's store. Inside, he glanced from the nearly empty shelves to the barrels that lined the wall. His eyes widened when he saw the price of flour, and he hoped the cornmeal they'd brought from Riverview would last a long time.

After the storekeeper measured a pint of molasses into an old woman's jar and took the handful of Confederate bills she counted out, Edward asked him about the salt. The man looked over his spectacles and said, "Son, there hasn't been any salt for sale in this town since I can remember. I thought everybody knew that."

"I—I'm sorry," Edward said, backing away.

"I'm sorry, too," the storekeeper said. "What isn't scarce as hen's teeth costs more than most folks can pay."

Edward wondered how sorry the man really was. He'd heard his aunt complain that unscrupulous merchants held goods back, waiting for prices to rise still higher and for the citizens to be desperate enough to pay almost anything for them. "This war is making evil men rich while innocent people suffer," Aunt Charlotte had raged.

Edward's eyes strayed to the flour barrels again, and he asked, "You think prices will go up still more now that the Yankees have dug in east of the city?"

"I know they will," the storekeeper said. "And each time they cut another rail line, the shortages will be worse."

Now Edward understood why Uncle Gilbert had said everything depended on keeping the trains running, understood why Father hadn't come to see them. He imagined his father leading a cavalry patrol, saw him round a curve and catch sight of Yankees prying rails from the track ahead of them. Leaning low, Father spurred his horse forward, pulling his carbine from its holster and aiming it at the Yankee sentinel. The blue-coated sentinel raised his rifle, and—

" . . . anything else you need, young man?"

Blinking, Edward shook his head, and as a servant carrying a basket came into the store, he made his way out and headed for the army headquarters to read the casualty lists again.

On his way home half an hour later, Edward's thoughts turned to Jocasta. She'd deliberately sent him on a wild-goose chase and made him look foolish in front of the storekeeper, too. Well, she'd be sorry. He'd find some way to settle his score with her, some way that would teach her a lesson.

Edward trudged uphill, deep in thought, oblivious to the perspiration dampening his shirt and trickling down his cheeks. Suddenly he said aloud, "That's it! That's what I'll do." It was a plan worthy of Simon, he thought with satisfaction.

Minutes later he was climbing the stairs to the house. Becky, who had been waiting with her face pressed to the window, ran to meet him, and Jocasta quickly appeared to ask, "You git my salt?"

Edward shook his head. "Mr. Endicott said he's getting some in the morning. He figures folks will be lining up to buy it."

Jocasta's eyebrows rose, but before she could reply, Mother and Aunt Charlotte came in after their day of volunteer work at one of the hospitals. Mother's face was drawn, and Aunt Charlotte's mouth was set in a grim line. Becky ran and threw her arms around first her mother and then her aunt, and after Edward had greeted them both he said, "I went out for a while this afternoon, Mother." He heard Jocasta draw a quick breath, and he added, "If it's safe enough for you and Aunt Charlotte and Mary Beth to be out, it's safe enough for me."

Edward braced himself for an argument, but his mother simply nodded and then slowly climbed the stairs, holding tightly to the curved banister. Edward stared after her, and Aunt Charlotte slipped an arm around his shoulders and said, "She'll be all right. It was a terrible day at the hospital. All those poor wounded men and the fear that the next one you saw might be—" She broke off and pressed the back of her hand to her mouth. But then she squared her shoulders and said, "I'll go look in on your mother." Her spine was straight as she went upstairs.

When Edward opened his eyes the next morning the first thing he heard was artillery fire and the second was the sound of the back door closing. He crept along the upstairs hall and reached the back window in time to see Jocasta going out the gate, a basket on her arm. She was on her way to Mr. Endicott's store, prepared to wait until opening time to get salt, Edward thought, a smile spreading across his face. His plan had worked!

Later, when he went downstairs, Aunt Charlotte was setting the table for breakfast. She looked up and said, "I can't imagine where Jocasta could be. Have you seen her this morning, Edward?"

"I think she's gone off someplace," he hedged.

"Nonsense. Jocasta is the soul of responsibility. She'd never leave the house without telling me, and she'd certainly not go out before breakfast."

Edward stared at the floor. It was one thing to get even with Jocasta for tricking him, and quite another to get her in trouble. His heart sank when Aunt Charlotte said, "I have a notion you know more about this than you're telling me, young man."

What should he say? The room was silent except for the clink of silver as his aunt moved around the table. Was she waiting for him to answer, or was she showing her displeasure by not speaking to him? Edward was relieved when the back door opened and a moment later Jocasta appeared, her face stony.

"Where have you been, Jocasta?" Aunt Charlotte asked sternly.

"I'se been waitin' for Marse Endicott's store to open so's I could git salt. I fergit to tell you las' evenin', somebody done tol' me he gonna have salt dis mornin'. But dey was wrong."

"Who on earth told you a thing like that, Jocasta?"

"One of de devil's own mischief makers, Miss Charlotte," Jocasta hissed. The hairs along the back of Edward's neck began to rise, but she didn't look in his direction. "I have de breakfas' ready soon," she said.

Edward felt his aunt's eyes on him, and when he saw her disapproving look he stammered, "I—I'm sorry for the trouble I caused, Aunt Charlotte."

"See that nothing like this happens again," she said coldly, and then she, too, headed for the kitchen.

Edward watched her go, sorry to have upset her. But then he grinned. "'One of de devil's own mischief makers,'" he mimicked. Jocasta would think twice before she pulled another trick on him.

EARLY JULY, 1864

Edward was carefully pouring a little water around each plant in the drought-parched garden when Michael called, "Hey, Edward, want to see if them blackberries in the woods along the river are ripe yet?"

"Sure, soon as I finish here." If it was all right to water the garden on Sunday, he figured he could pick berries, too.

Long before the boys reached the river, they were damp with sweat. Edward wondered if it was the heat or something else that was keeping Michael so quiet, but before he could ask what was wrong, the other boy spoke.

"You know what day tomorrow is?"

"Of course—it's Monday."

Michael made an impatient gesture. "The *date,* not the day."

"July fourth," Edward said quickly, wondering how he was supposed to know what Michael meant. And then he understood.

Michael nodded. "The Fourth of July used to be even better 'n Christmas. Picnics, an' lemonade, an'—"

"Races and games," Edward interrupted. "And maybe a band concert, too."

"I used to look forward to it all year."

"Someday we'll have an Independence Day of our own, Michael," Edward said, noticing with disappointment that the berry bushes had been picked clean. "An Independence Day for the Confederacy."

"I wish it was today," Michael said as he threw a stick into the river and watched the current swirl it away.

Edward thought of the line of trenches the Yankees had dug outside the city, and he didn't answer.

"I hear the home guard's supposed to be ready tomorrow 'cause General Grant might be plannin' an attack in honor of the Fourth," Michael said.

"Duncan's sure he is," Edward said, trying to sound matter-of-fact in spite of the fear that gnawed at him. At least there were more soldiers manning the trenches now, he told himself. He wondered whether Michael was thinking about how his brother was killed when the home guard fought against the Yankee cavalry the month before.

Michael squinted up at Edward and asked, "How come he's so sure?" When Edward looked at him blankly he repeated impatiently, "How come your brother's so sure the Yankees are gonna attack?"

Edward shrugged. He didn't want to think about Duncan's solemn announcement that the Yankees probably hoped to mark tomorrow's anniversary of the fall of Vicksburg by taking Petersburg. Even Aunt Charlotte's disapproving look hadn't kept Duncan from pointing out that it was Grant's army that had besieged Vicksburg, and that Vicksburg had held out for less than seven weeks.

Glancing at the lengthening shadows, Edward said, "I'd better start on back so I'm not late for supper. Mother and Aunt Charlotte are awfully cranky lately—must be the heat."

"Or else they're worried that the Yankees are gonna attack tomorrow," Michael said glumly. "Lots more people have left town for fear they will." He bent to pick up his empty berry baskets.

In spite of the heat of the early evening, Edward shivered. Michael wasn't much fun anymore, he thought as he said good-bye. . . .

The next morning, Edward woke with a start. He sat up, his heart racing, and struggled to make sense of what he was hearing. *BADOOM!* Could this be the Union attack everyone feared? *BADOOM!* No, not with only one gun firing—*BADOOM!*—and firing evenly spaced reports. Edward held his breath and waited for another. When it came, he knew he was hearing a Union salute in honor of the Fourth. He gritted his teeth and counted.

". . . nineteen . . . twenty . . . twenty-one." *BADOOM!* Twenty-two? Caught off guard, Edward decided he must have counted wrong. *BADOOM! BADOOM!* He buried his head under the pillow, sure now that it would be a hundred-gun salute.

When it was finally over, Edward's whole face ached from clenching his teeth. He dressed quickly and joined the rest of the family in the dining room in time to hear his sister ask, "Will the courthouse bell ring if the Yankees come today?"

Edward saw the women exchange quick glances, and then Aunt Charlotte said, "The bell rings whenever anything happens that we all need to know about, so you mustn't worry if you hear it. And you mustn't worry if the Yankees do come into the city someday, Becky. They aren't going to harm women and children."

In a small voice, Mary Beth asked, "What will we do? If they come, that is?"

"Lock the doors so they can't steal anything and close the shutters so we don't have to look at them," Aunt Charlotte said. Then she gave Duncan such a fierce look that he seemed to think better of any objections he had been about to make.

The day dragged by. Edward and Mary Beth played endless games of cribbage while Becky watched and Duncan paced from room to room, sometimes peering out a window at the army wagons that rumbled along the cobblestone street. But the sounds of band music in the distance reassured Edward that the Yankees were marking their Independence Day with celebrations instead of with an attack on Petersburg.

Later, as the family sat on the side porch at dusk, Aunt Charlotte said, "So the great Fourth of July assault on the city was only a rumor. See that you remember this the next time everyone says something terrible is about to happen."

The words were scarcely out of her mouth when Edward heard a keening sound and saw a dark shape move up the porch steps and collapse at his aunt's feet. "Is that you, Jocasta? Get up this instant!" Aunt Charlotte said. "Whatever is the matter with you?"

Edward could hardly believe that the woman huddled in front of his aunt was the sharp-tongued servant who scorned him and frightened Becky. He watched in amazement while Jocasta pulled herself together enough to say, "I'se sorry, Miss Charlotte, but I jus' foun' out dem Yankee gonna blow us all to kingdom come."

"Stop this nonsense at once," Aunt Charlotte scolded. "If the Yankees could do that, they already would have."

The frightened woman shook her head. "Dey not ready yet. Dey still diggin'." She threw her apron up over her face and wept noisily. It took several minutes for Jocasta's hysteria to subside enough that she could tell them what she'd heard: The Yankees were planning to blow up the city by tunneling beneath it and filling the tunnel with explosives.

"That's preposterous, Jocasta!" exclaimed Aunt Charlotte. "Go inside and don't let me hear another word about this. Ever!" Then she turned to the others and said, "You young people should forget what you just heard. It's worse than gossip."

"It's probably a story the Yankees planted to frighten us and lower our morale," Duncan said. He turned to Mary Beth and warned, "Anyone who repeats it will be helping the enemy."

Mary Beth tossed her head and looked away, and Edward felt a flash of sympathy for his cousin. . . .

Several days later, the rumor surfaced again, and after Becky went to bed, Mary Beth repeated the conversation she and her friend Agatha had overheard between two soldiers outside the library. "One of them said he could hear scraping sounds under the ground when he was on picket duty. At first his friend said that wasn't possible, but he didn't sound so sure after he found out a Pennsylvania unit was opposite them."

"What difference does that make?" Edward asked.

"A lot of Pennsylvanians are miners," Mary Beth explained. Horrified, Edward looked from his cousin to the shocked faces of his mother and Aunt Charlotte. Then he turned to Duncan and saw that his brother seeemed to be deep in thought.

"So," Mary Beth went on, her voice hardening, "I guess our resident military strategist was wrong about Jocasta's story being something the Yankees made up to frighten us."

Duncan ignored his cousin's baiting and said slowly, "You know, the Union line is pretty close to ours in a couple of places, like on that hill by the cemetery. They might be trying to tunnel under our fortifications so they can get into the city." Then, noticing Jocasta standing in the doorway looking smug, he added, "But there's no way they could dig a tunnel under Petersburg."

That night, Edward dreamed of Union troops pouring out of a groundhog hole in the garden. Jocasta beat them with her broom while he tried unsuccessfully to roll a rock over the hole to stem the tide.

JULY 30, 1864

Simon lay in the grass on a low hill well behind the Union lines. Propped on his elbows with his chin cupped in his hands, he faced the Confederate battery Ambrose had pointed out to him and stared into the darkness, waiting.

A rooster crowed in the distance, and Simon frowned. It was almost daybreak—had something gone wrong? Already the darkness was thinning in the east, and the stark outline of the Rebel battery was slowly becoming visible. Simon thought of leaving, but he didn't want to miss his chance to see the Union army, with Negro soldiers in the lead, break through the Petersburg defenses.

Those Rebels wouldn't know what hit them when the

gunpowder packed into the tunnel under their fort exploded, Simon thought, marveling at how far the Pennsylvanians had dug through the earth.

Soon, streaks of pale pink colored the sky near the horizon, and a bird trilled its waking song. Something must have gone wrong, Simon thought uneasily.

And then it happened. The earth trembled, and in the half-light, the Confederate battery seemed to silently crumple inward. Moments later, Simon heard a deafening roar and saw flashes of fire. He clapped the field glasses to his face in time to see cannon and men and wagons and great chunks of earth thrown high into the air, part of a huge, billowing cloud of dust. While Simon watched, scarcely breathing, the cloud spread out in all directions and then rained its load back to earth. He stared as bodies arched to the ground in slow cartwheels; then, sickened, he closed his eyes and buried his face in his arms.

Suddenly the ground beneath Simon shook and the air around him seemed to vibrate as a blast of artillery fire echoed along the Union lines. He squeezed his eyes shut and pressed his body against the earth until the shelling subsided to a continuous low thunder.

Slowly, Simon opened his eyes and reached for the field glasses. He blinked in amazement when the scene leaped toward him. Through the haze of dust and smoke he could make out a jagged hole that gaped like an open wound—a long gash exposing the red clay below the earth's dusty surface where only minutes ago the Rebel fort had stood.

Turning away from the site of the explosion, Simon's eyes swept the space between the lines, searching for the Negro troops who had been chosen to lead the attack on the city. At first he saw only confusion, but finally blue-clad figures straggled forward. In the gathering light Simon could see that though the soldiers were deeply tanned from weeks of exposure to the sun, they were white men. He cursed under his breath and thought of the weeks that Ambrose and the others had drilled, preparing for this moment. How proud they'd been that their unit would be the first to enter Petersburg after the blast leveled the fort and opened the way into the city!

What could have gone wrong? And why were the white soldiers milling around the edge of the gaping hole? Simon watched in disbelief as they began to slide down into the giant crater instead of breaching the enemy's line. "Our men wouldn't of done a stupid thing like that," he muttered angrily. "They'd of marched right into Petersburg, like they wanted to the last time."

Watching the scene of confusion, he saw with dismay that the Rebels who had fled the explosion were moving forward now. When they began firing into the crater Simon's stomach roiled, and he buried his face in his arms again and lay flat on the dry grass. But he couldn't block out the battle sounds—the roar of artillery, bursts of rifle fire, distant shouts and cries. A sense of certainty settled over him, a conviction that again the Union army had missed its chance to take the city. . . .

When the tired, beaten men began to straggle into camp, Simon lit the fire he'd laid. A cast-iron cauldron hung from a tripod, full of water to be heated for washing, and the coffeepot sat ready to be surrounded by the first coals that could be raked out.

Folks said a watched pot wouldn't boil, Simon thought

some time later, but steam had been rising from the coffee pot for quite a while now. Though soldiers were streaming into camp, all of them were white. Finally, Simon could stand it no longer, and he forced himself to go and speak to one of them.

"Please, suh," he said, "where all de colored soldier, suh?"

The man's face was smoke-stained, his eyes red-rimmed, and speaking seemed to be a great effort for him. "They went forward singing," he said at last, "but I never seen none of 'em come back."

"You think dey pris'ner, suh?"

The man shook his head. "From what I hear, them Rebels wouldn't let no colored men surrender," he said. "Shot 'em point-blank, or else beat 'em down with their rifle butts."

A wave of fear swept over Simon. Had *Ambrose* been shot point blank or beaten down by Rebels? Was that why he hadn't come back?

"It's a terrible thing," the soldier said quietly, almost as though he were talking to himself. "Terrible," he repeated as he continued on his way.

Simon felt numb. Weeks ago, when the soldiers stormed the Rebel earthworks, he'd feared for Ambrose, but this time he hadn't even worried. He'd let himself be lulled by his brother's assurance that far more soldiers died of disease in camps than were killed on the battlefield. But now, instead of taking Petersburg, Ambrose and the others might be—

Don't even think it, Simon told himself. He turned and walked slowly back to the campsite, muttering, "He'll be back. He can take care of himself." Not knowing what else to do, Simon sat down and stared into the dying fire, watching the steam rising from the coffee pot and not thinking at all, until he was suddenly aware of someone beside him. "Ambrose!" he cried, filled with relief. But it wasn't Ambrose. It was Luke, and he was alone.

"Ambrose ain't comin' back," Luke said dully, "an' de other ain't, neither. Dey dead. Only reason I'se alive is, I run." He drew a long, shuddering breath. "When dem Rebel charge at us hollerin' 'Kill de niggers,' I run. Lot of us did, an' when all dem white soldier saw us runnin' back, dey turn tail an' run, too."

Simon stared at Luke, unwilling to believe what he'd said.

"It all dem general fault!" Luke burst out. "Dey sen' dose white soldier dat don't know what to do 'nstead of lettin' us go first an' do what we practice all dat time. Dat why we not in de city now. Dat why yo' brother dead."

Tears welled up in Simon's eyes and he forced back a sob, remembering all the times Ambrose had scolded him when he was small, cuffing him and saying scornfully, "You know cryin' don't help none." His hand trembled so much when he poured Luke's coffee that he splashed the hot liquid on his own thumb, but the pain couldn't distract him from the fact that Ambrose was dead.

What was he going to do? Ambrose had said to stay with the army, but that didn't mean he had to stay right here. Blinking back tears, Simon stuffed his few belongings into a sack and walked away, leaving Luke staring into the fire, his coffee untouched beside him.

Simon didn't trust Luke, had seen his shifty eyes linger

longingly on the field glasses and knew that it was only because of Ambrose that they hadn't disappeared. Why couldn't Ambrose have been the one who came back?

Simon walked slowly, his eyes on the ground, and at the edge of the camp, he automatically turned toward Riverview. He trudged for mile after mile, choking on the dust stirred up by passing wagons and riders until his mouth and throat were dry as cotton and he could feel grit on his teeth. The merciless sun beat down on him, adding to his misery. *Why did Ambrose have to die?*

At last Simon reached the village of City Point, but with its streets full of soldiers and the homes taken over as officers' quarters, it wasn't at all the place he'd known. And Riverview! Besides tents as far as he could see, large frame buildings had sprung up everywhere. Taken aback by the frenetic activity, Simon stopped and stared. Suddenly a hand on his shoulder spun him around and he found himself looking up into the face of one of the provost guard—the military police.

"I—I ain't doin' nothin', suh."

"I can see that. You think we should feed you for nothing?"

Confused, Simon stammered, "I j-jus' got here, suh."

The officer gave him a long hard look, and apparently his dusty appearance convinced the man that he was telling the truth. "I'll show you to the contraband camp, and you can find someone to take you in. Tomorrow morning, report for work on the wharf. You're sturdy enough to be a water boy."

Water! "Please, suh, can I git some water now?"

The man gestured to a nearby pump, and Simon slaked his thirst and then pumped water over his head to cool himself until the officer shouted, "I don't have all day, boy!"

Simon followed the man past a long row of workshops and then a sawmill, confused by the strangeness of everything he saw. At last the haphazard jumble of crude shelters that made up the crowded contraband camp came into view, and the provost guard motioned him toward it. Simon's heart fell. Even at this distance he could hear the wails of small children, and he half wished he'd stayed and taken his chances with Luke.

Smoke rose from fires under cauldrons of boiling water where some of the women did the soldiers' laundry. As Simon drew closer he could see the set look on the faces of the laundresses who stirred the clothing with wooden paddles. Inside the compound, old men watched Simon with veiled eyes as he made his way past their shacks, and half-naked small children stared as he passed, but he ignored them. They were all strangers, and he was hoping to find a familiar face.

Suddenly he stopped. Not a familiar face, but a voice he once knew as well as his own mother's. "Aunt Lou," he whispered, and he followed the sound to an old woman who sat on a box outside a makeshift shelter, crooning as she cradled a fretful infant. She would take him in.

"You 'member me, Aunt Lou?" Simon asked, moving closer when she stopped singing and peered at him. "I'se Simon. My ma—"

"Yo' ma Patty Sue, God res' her soul. 'Course I 'member you. Never yet fergit no babe I care for, even when dey go off to de Great House an' fergit me," the old woman said, her eyes like smoldering coals in her wrinkled face. Before Simon could reply she added scornfully, "Wi' dem white folk gone, didn't take you long to 'member ol' Lou."

This wasn't going at all like he had planned, Simon thought, but he could win her over. "You know dat ain't so, Aunt Lou," he protested. "It done took me 'most three month."

Aunt Lou patted the whimpering baby on the back. "Three month on his own an' den he come crawlin' back. Mus' be a tale to tell dere, so set down an' tell it."

Relief surged through Simon when he realized the old woman wouldn't turn him away, but as he looked into her eager face he knew he couldn't talk about what had happened to Ambrose. Not yet. And not with Aunt Lou's eyes on him. He'd have to tell her after dark, when he could stare into the fire. "I'se too tired," he said. "I tell you after dat one ma take it 'way."

The old woman shrugged, and Simon spread his blanket just outside her shelter and lay down on it, his back to Aunt Lou and the curious children who had come to stare. Through the numbness that settled over him, he heard an old man's quavery voice ask, "Who dat young'un, Lou? Where he come from?"

At that instant, Simon knew he wasn't going to tell about Ambrose, wasn't going to tell about the explosion at the Rebel fort this morning or the battle that followed. He'd have to make up some tale to satisfy Aunt Lou, because his grief and the horror of what he'd seen weren't going to become entertainment for the contraband camp. Not tonight. Not ever.

In Petersburg, throngs of people lined the streets, waiting to see the Yankee prisoners marched by.

"They're comin'," Michael said excitedly.

Edward nodded, tense with anticipation, and as the strains of "Dixie" reached his ears, he stepped farther into the street and craned his neck to see if the band was in sight.

The crowd cheered as the musicians approached, but when the first of the prisoners taken after the explosion came into view, the mood changed. Edward wasn't surprised when Michael began to throw pebbles at the Yankees, but he was shocked to see a woman run out and spit at one of the prisoners.

Another woman taunted, "You Yankees won't look half so well fed when you've been eating like our boys do for a while."

Edward noticed that the Yankees did look well fed, and well dressed, too. He thought of the thin, ragged Confederate soldiers, and with a rush of anger he bent down to scoop up a handful of small stones. His heart racing, he stood poised to throw. He waited impatiently for a gray-haired soldier to pass and then for a wounded man to limp by. As he searched the line of marchers for a target, Edward saw that most of the men kept their eyes straight ahead. But one young soldier stared curiously at the people who lined the streets.

He'd teach that Yankee to stare at the women of Petersburg,

Edward thought, taking aim. But as the man passed, his eyes met Edward's, and the boy's arm dropped to his side. Confused, Edward wondered how he would be able to shoot an enemy when he was a soldier if he couldn't even throw a rock—a pebble!—at one now.

"C'mon, Edward," Michael urged, squatting down to gather more ammunition. "Make 'em pay for what they done."

Instantly, Edward relived the terror he'd felt when he was shaken awake by the rattling of windows and a roar that sounded like a train steaming through his room. He'd make them pay, all right! Blindly, he hurled one stone after another, until someone grabbed his arm and almost jerked him off his feet. Catching his balance, he looked up into his aunt's blazing eyes.

"Don't you ever do a cowardly thing like that again!"

"But they're our enemies," Edward protested.

"They're our *prisoners,"* Aunt Charlotte corrected firmly, releasing his arm, "and you'll treat them the way you'd want your father to be treated if *he* were in *their* hands."

Father in Yankee hands? Edward felt a chill, and suddenly he didn't want to watch the captured soldiers any longer. His eyes on the ground, he started for home, walking against the flow of prisoners and their guards.

What if Father had been captured by the Yankees? What if he were in one of their prisons right now? Maybe that was why he hadn't come to see them. Maybe instead of riding hard with the sun on his face and the wind in his hair, Father was crowded into a dark, damp prison cell somewhere in the North.

"No," Edward whispered, "Father would never be taken

prisoner." He blinked away the image of his father, saber in one hand and carbine in the other, his back against an abandoned barn, surrounded by a dozen Yankees. "No!" Edward said aloud, turning toward Confederate headquarters to check the casualty lists.

Jocasta was sweeping the front porch when he finally reached his aunt's house, and she sent a cloud of dust in his direction. Coughing, Edward glared at her, but her back was to him as she grumbled about "some folks' chillun who's always underfoot." He brushed himself off and went inside.

Voices were coming from the sitting room, and Edward hesitated in the hallway, listening to Duncan's eager words. "It's the least I can do, Mother. You know the army can't spare soldiers to guard the thousands of prisoners we took after the explosion."

Straining his ears, Edward heard his mother say, "You'll be making a real contribution to the Confederate cause, Duncan, and I know how important that is to you."

Edward slipped into the parlor so he wouldn't have to see the triumphant look on his brother's face when Duncan came out of the sitting room. Some triumph, Edward thought scornfully. Mother only agreed so quickly because she knew guarding prisoners was a safe way for Duncan to play soldier.

AUGUST 9, 1864, AND THE FOLLOWING DAY

As Simon worked the creaking pump handle, he wondered what Edward would think if he saw

Riverview now. If it weren't for the Great House standing among the army tents, *he* wouldn't believe this was the plantation where he'd spent his whole life.

Water gushed over the rim of the wooden bucket, and Simon lifted it aside and filled another one. He hooked the buckets onto his yoke and settled it on his shoulders, then started off, walking carefully. The more water he spilled, the sooner he'd have to make this trip again. He wondered how many times he'd made it since he'd come back when Ambrose was killed more than a week ago. "Don't think about it," Simon whispered. "Just don't think about that day at all."

At the edge of the bluff he stopped to look down on the teeming wharves below him, still half expecting to see only the small steamship landing—all that had been there three months before. But after the Negro soldiers left Riverview to march toward Petersburg, General Grant had come and set up his headquarters where Miss Emily's lawn used to be. And then the general had taken over all of City Point and made it the supply base for his whole army, with bakeries and huge commissaries, and even more.

Simon's eyes traveled over the barges that lined the wharves, waiting for their cargoes to be transferred to the warehouses the general had ordered built. With General Grant in charge, the North couldn't help but win the war, Simon thought as he started down the wooden steps to the wharf.

"Water boy!"

Simon hurried toward the heavyset sergeant whose men were building another warehouse. Filling a dipper, he handed it to the officer. The man drank, then dropped the empty dipper and turned away. Simon stooped to retrieve it, wondering how the sergeant would react if he knew he'd drunk from the contrabands' dipper.

Everyone knew that the bucket and dipper in a water boy's right hand was for the white soldiers, the one in his left for the Negroes. But only Simon knew that each time he filled the buckets, he switched them. It made him feel good—almost powerful—to put something over on the white men who ignored him while they drank.

"Water boy! Hey, water boy!"

Simon moved farther down the wharf and filled the dipper in the bucket on the left. Thirsty men gathered around him, and while they drank, his eyes were on the feverish activity along the waterfront. When the Negro workers had drunk their fill, they set to work again. Simon watched them form a line from a munitions barge to a wagon on the wharf and then toss crates from one to another until the last man swung them up to a worker in the wagon. Lulled by the men's rhythmic motions and the monotony of the work song they sang, Simon was startled by a shout.

"You, there—water boy! Stop your gawking!" An angry-looking officer was bearing down on Simon with his fist raised.

Leaving the yoke and buckets behind, he dashed away. He'd never been beaten when he was a slave, and he certainly wasn't going to be hit now that he was free. Simon snaked his way through the throng of workmen and darted between two loaded wagons. He had almost reached the steps that led to the top of the bluff when a burst of hot air knocked him flat, roaring as it rushed past.

Simon pressed himself against the wharf as a deafening

blast echoed off the bluff and made the boards beneath him tremble. When he opened his eyes, the air was filled with flying bullets and exploding shells from the munitions barge, and to Simon's horror, a huge wooden beam was sailing toward him, end over end.

Almost paralyzed by fear, Simon covered his head with his arms. He felt the shock as one end of the beam struck the wharf, and then something hit his legs. The other end of the beam had crashed against the bluff, and clods of dirt it dislodged were raining down on him.

Simon scrambled to safety and then looked around, trying to figure out what had happened. He gasped when he saw that the barge and the wagon where the contrabands had been loading boxes of ammunition had disappeared. Other barges were ablaze, and flames had spread along the wharf to the warehouses. As Simon watched, aghast, the fire inched toward him.

The wharf shook under the pounding of running feet, and men in uniform raced past Simon. He watched numbly as some of them began to carry the wounded to safety and others tried to battle the blaze. His ears ringing painfully from the blast, Simon stared first at the spreading cloud of smoke and then at the place where the munitions barge had been anchored. If that angry officer hadn't hollered at him, he'd be—

Quickly, Simon turned from the scene of devastation and made his way toward the steps that led to the top of the bluff. His eyes widened when he saw that the trees along the edge had been stripped nearly bare by the force of the explosion. He looked toward the Great House and was relieved to see that except for shattered windows, it had survived the blast.

Simon craned his neck and looked toward General Grant's tent. The Union leader stood in front of it, a cigar clamped between his teeth. He seemed to be surveying the clutter of metal, splintered wood, and other debris that had rained down and now littered the ground around him. Amid the scene of panic and confusion, he looked solid and strong.

Reassured, Simon headed toward the contraband camp. Don't think about what happened back there, he told himself. "Won't do no good to think about it," he said loudly. He kept his mind blank as he walked by row after row of enlisted men's shelter tents that lined neatly laid out "streets," and then he came to the officers' cabinlike wall tents, shaded by evergreen boughs laid across wooden frames.

If he were still the lieutenant's darky, Simon thought, he could be sitting under an evergreen canopy somewhere this very minute. But here he was, dragging himself toward the hodgepodge of shacks in the area set aside for Negroes who had fled their plantations to follow the Union army.

His luck had run out when Ambrose was killed, Simon decided. Life had been good until then—first with the lieutenant, then with Uncle Hap, and finally with Ambrose and his friends. But now life was hard. Even field hands hadn't worked longer hours than he was working now, and compared to the crowded contraband camp, the slave quarters where the field hands lived had been luxurious.

The slave cabins were gone now, though, torn down and

used for firewood. Simon hoped the soldiers wouldn't ruin the Great House. That had been more of a home to him than the quarters—for almost as long as he remembered, he'd slept on a pallet in Edward's room. Edward had kept insisting on that until at last Miss Emily agreed.

Simon had been glad to escape the small, dark slave cabin with its dirt floor, but he hadn't liked it that another boy's wishes could change *his* life just because the other boy was white. That was when he'd begun to understand what slavery meant. To understand that Edward owned him.

Simon's steps slowed as he neared the contraband camp and saw that the washerwomen had left their tubs and were staring up at the sky. Looking back, he saw a billowing cloud of flame-edged smoke that hung in the sky above the wharf, and he quickly turned away from it and made his way toward Aunt Lou's shack. He could already hear the baby she cared for squalling. No wonder the other washerwomen wouldn't let the mother keep it with her while she worked.

"Lord o' mercy, what happen to you, boy?" the old woman cried when she saw Simon. "You jus' cover wi' dirt!"

Curious eyes turned in his direction, and Simon knew that if he told the story of what had just happened, he would have an instant audience. A few months ago, he would have found that irresistible, but then his stories were wickedly funny ones, stories about Miss Emily or Marse Duncan, and sometimes even stories about the coachman, Isaac, who thought himself so grand. Those stories had made the people in the quarters laugh, had kept them from thinking he was uppity because he was a house servant, but this was different. He didn't want to think about what had happened on the wharf, much less talk about it.

"I'se gonna wash, Aunt Lou," Simon said, picking up the nearly empty water bucket and heading toward the pump. . . .

It was late when Simon lowered himself onto the blanket-covered pile of straw that was his bed, but in spite of his exhaustion, he couldn't sleep. His body was sore and his ears ached, and the noise in the compound seemed even worse than usual as people mourned the victims of the explosion.

Carefully, Simon turned over, conscious of the field glasses beneath him where no one could steal them while he slept. Tonight he'd seen one of the younger men eye them with longing, just as Luke had, and to be safe, before he slid the glasses under his blanket Simon had tied the strap around his upper arm.

A child cried out as though it had wakened from a bad dream, and then Simon heard muttered curses from some closer neighbor roused by the sound. How he missed the quiet of the army camp after taps, missed the predictability of always knowing what would come next. Here in the contraband camp, he never knew what to expect. He hated it—hated the noise and commotion—and if it weren't for the curfew, he would leave this very minute.

He'd have to wait till morning, but as soon as it was light, he'd leave the confusion of the contraband camp and the danger of the munitions wharf behind him, Simon decided. He was free, after all. He could walk away from here just like he'd walked away from the lieutenant, just like he'd walked away from Uncle Hap and then from Luke.

Yes, as soon as it was light, he'd roll up his blanket and leave this place, slip out and be on his way without any fuss. He'd stick with the army, like Ambrose told him to, and he'd be all right. He'd find some way to earn his keep. He had so far, hadn't he?

The sun beat down on Simon's head the next afternoon and he felt as though he were breathing dust instead of air. A spattering of rifle fire made him realize how close he'd come to the front line, and still he hadn't found anyone who needed a boy to work for him. He was wondering if he should have stayed at the contraband camp when he heard someone shouting.

"Sebastian? Seb-as-tian!" It was a huge white man, his skin leathery from exposure to the sun and his shirt plastered to him with sweat. He stood beside a blacksmith's forge in a makeshift shed formed by a few upright logs and roofed with wilted pine boughs, part of a wagon repair shop behind the Union lines.

The man looked angry, but he didn't look mean, Simon decided. "Please, suh," he said, walking toward the blacksmith, "if Sebastian done run off, I can work your bellows." He held his breath while the man looked him over. "I used to help out at de forge on de plantation 'fore I run off," he lied.

The smith pointed to the lever that worked his huge bellows and said, "Get to work then, boy. We'll see if you last any longer than the last one."

Simon rested his weight on the lever and heard the *whoosh!* of air rush out. The surge of heat when the blast of oxygen hit the coals was almost overpowering, and he understood at once why Sebastian had left. But Simon knew he'd stay—at least till he found something better. The work couldn't be much hotter than carrying water all day in the blazing sun, and it wouldn't be nearly as hard. And best of all, he had left the contraband camp behind. Now he could simply roll out his blanket at the back of the blacksmith shed each night.

Through the shimmering heat waves Simon looked across the field that lay parched and baking in the late afternoon sun. He thought of the green lawns that had surrounded the Great House before the army came, and of the shaded gazebo—a perfect place to enjoy the breeze from the river. On summer afternoons, he and Edward would sometimes sit there playing cribbage or dominoes, and Elberta would bring them cool glasses of lemonade.

Simon pumped the bellows again and wondered if Edward's life had changed as much as his had.

MID-AUGUST, 1864

Edward shut his sketch pad and slipped his mechanical pencil into his pocket when Michael called to him from the back gate.

"Want to go down to the swimmin' hole?" Michael asked.

"I can't," Edward said, disappointed. "I have to keep an eye on the garden." Michael looked puzzled, so he explained, "My aunt wants me to make sure nobody steals her vegetables. Yesterday a couple of soldiers picked a whole row of green beans before Jocasta chased them off. Want to stay and play mumblety-peg?"

"Sure," Michael said, pulling out his pocketknife and coming into the yard. "Ma don't want me swimmin' alone."

A few minutes later the gate creaked, and the boys looked up from their game to see a ragged soldier slip into the yard and make his way to the hills of summer squash. Edward scrambled to his feet and shouted, "Hey! What do you think you're doing?"

The soldier wheeled around, and Edward saw the startled face of a blond boy who didn't look much older than Duncan. "I—I was—" He paused, and his shoulders sagged. "I guess I was going to steal some vegetables from your mama's garden," he admitted, his eyes on the ground. Then, blushing, he said earnestly, "I'm sorry—it's just that after weeks of hardtack and salt pork, you start to crave something fresh grown." He turned toward the gate. "I—I'm sorry," he repeated.

"Wait!" Edward called after him. "I'll give you a couple of those squash and some greens to cook with your salt pork."

The young soldier's eyes lit up, and he waited while Edward picked two of the largest squash and began to pinch off the outside leaves of the turnip tops. The soldier was stuffing the squash in his haversack when the back door of the house opened and Jocasta burst out.

"Run!" Edward said, shoving the greens at the young man and pushing him toward the gate.

"Puttin' de likes of you out here ain't no better 'n settin' de fox to guard de henhouse!" Jocasta raged, shaking her broom in Edward's face. His heart beat faster, but he held his ground, knowing she wouldn't dare hit him. "You git! Jus' git out of here!" she said through clenched teeth. "I knowed de minute I done set eyes on you dat you was useless. Useless!"

Stung by her words, Edward turned to Michael and said, "Let's go swimming." He needed to cool off, in more ways than one.

The soldier was waiting for them at the corner. "Sorry I got you boys in trouble," he said. "Don't worry—I'll not come back."

Prompted by a combination of his anger toward Jocasta and an instant liking for the young soldier, Edward said, "Next time, go to the front door and ask for Miss Charlotte, and my aunt will give you some vegetables."

"You think your aunt really will do that?" Michael asked as they turned downhill.

Edward nodded. "She'll look at him and think of Wesley, her son who's fighting in the Shenandoah Valley, and she'll *want* to feed him." That will show Jocasta, he added silently.

It was late afternoon when Edward and Michael left the swimming hole and headed home. They parted at Aunt Charlotte's back gate, and when Edward lifted the latch he was startled by the loud jangle of cowbells. He understood at once when Jocasta came charging out of the summer kitchen waving a knife and screeching, "You stay 'way from dat garden, you hear me?"

Edward hid his satisfaction when her arm dropped and she skidded to a stop. "I have no intention of going into the garden, Jocasta," he said coldly, and he watched her stalk away.

"I thought you were supposed to watch over the vegetables today," Mother said, looking up when Edward came into the sitting room where she and Aunt Charlotte were working.

"Jocasta hung a couple of bells on the gate so she'd know if anyone came in the yard," Edward answered. And then he asked in amazement, "Why are you cutting up the draperies?"

"For bandages," his aunt answered, winding a four-inch-wide strip of the flowered material into a roll.

This was as good a time as any to bring up his promise to the young soldier, Edward decided. "Aunt Charlotte," he said tentatively, "I did something today that might make you angry." His aunt raised her eyes to his, and Edward added in a rush, "I told a soldier I met that if he came to the door and asked for you, you'd give him some vegetables from the garden."

Before his aunt could answer, Mother asked, "Doesn't Charlotte do enough already? There's not a day goes by that she doesn't feed some poor hungry—"

"What was it that made you tell this particular soldier to come here, Edward?" Aunt Charlotte interrupted.

"He made me think of Wesley," Edward said, and turning to his mother he added, "He didn't look much older than Duncan."

The women's eyes met, and Aunt Charlotte said briskly, "One soldier isn't the whole army, after all. I'll tell Jocasta to fix a bundle for him if he comes when I'm not here."

Edward knew it had been wrong to play on his aunt's concern for Wesley in order to get back at Jocasta. He tried to convince himself that helping the young soldier was the important thing, but he still felt a little guilty.

The next morning Edward was so intent on his drawing that he barely noticed when Duncan came into the sitting room. He gave a start when his brother spoke.

"President Davis really told those Yankees this time," Duncan said, looking up from the newspaper. "Listen to this." He cleared his throat and began to read: " 'I tried in all my power to avert this war. I saw it coming, and for twelve years I worked day and night to prevent it, but I could not. And now it must go on till the last man of this generation falls in his tracks, and his children seize his musket and fight his battle, unless you acknowledge our right to self-government.' "

Edward stared at Duncan. He could see his brother's mouth move and hear the sound of his voice, but the rest of his words were drowned out by the echo of *children seize his musket and fight.* Edward gave a start when Duncan raised his eyes from the paper and said mockingly, "You're the scholar in the family, Edward. Can you tell me what that means?"

"What *what* means?" Edward asked, confused.

"Extermination. That's e-x—"

"It means total destruction," Edward said, glad that his voice didn't betray the dread he felt.

"Listen to this. 'We are fighting for Independence, and that, or extermination, we will have.'" Duncan's face was flushed with excitement when he looked up and said, "That message is as much for fainthearted southerners as it is for the Yankees, don't you think?" Before Edward could answer, the hall clock struck the half hour and Duncan was suddenly all business. "I'd better get down to the prison so I'm not late for guard duty."

Edward reached for the newspaper his brother had left on the table, and his eyes skimmed across the lines of closely spaced type until he found what he was looking for: *the last man of this generation falls . . . his children seize his musket . . .* Edward stared at the words. The Confederate president had really said that. It wasn't something Duncan made up to frighten him. Edward turned to a fresh page in his sketch pad and began to draw, trying to escape the fear that gripped him.

It was nearly noon by the time the drawing was finished. Edward was slumped in his chair, studying it, when Becky and Mary Beth came into the room.

"Oh, good! Another picture," Becky said. But when she looked at it, she exclaimed, "I don't like this one at all!"

"It's so violent," Mary Beth said, looking at it over Becky's shoulder.

Edward tried to see it through his cousin's eyes—the curved line of the enemy's earthworks broken by the barrels of cannon pointing toward the center of the picture, the boy bending over a fallen soldier and lifting a rifle from the man's lifeless hands.

"Look," said Becky, "I just noticed something strange about this picture—the boy and the dead man have the same face."

Mary Beth's voice shook as she said, "It's frightening. I don't like the way it makes me feel."

A sense of power surged through Edward. He'd forced his fear out of his mind and onto the paper, and from there into someone else's mind! He bent over the drawing and captioned it in neat letters: *The Last Man of His Generation Has Fallen and His Child Seizes His Musket.* The words went all the way across the paper.

Mary Beth gasped when she read what Edward had written. "That's downright morbid! Wherever did you get such an idea?"

"It's President Davis's idea. His plan, actually," Edward said. Now that his fear was gone, it was replaced by anger. Not the quick rush of anger he so often felt toward Duncan, but a cold, impersonal anger unlike anything he had ever known before. He handed the newspaper to his cousin and left the room.

Upstairs, Edward opened his sketch pad to a fresh page and centered the word *Extermination* at the bottom. Calling up in his mind's eye the image of the ruined market and the other buildings that had been destroyed by Yankee shells, he began to draw again. Would the Confederate president feel the same way if Yankees were shelling *Richmond*? If it were *his* father who went out on cavalry raids? If *he* were the child who would have to seize his dead father's musket?

"If I were president of the Confederate States of America, I wouldn't let my country be exterminated," Edward muttered.

EARLY SEPTEMBER, 1864

"Look, Edward," Becky said. "Jocasta's outside feeding the birds."

Edward joined his sister at the window to watch the servant toss crumbs to a small flock of pigeons. He scowled, thinking that he'd have asked for another piece of corn bread at breakfast if he'd known birds would eat it if he didn't.

"I think she's going to try to pet one!" Becky exclaimed.

Slowly, Jocasta leaned forward, and then with lightning speed she pounced on the boldest of the pigeons. A moment later, it lay crumpled in her basket, its neck wrung. The other birds scattered, but they ventured back when Jocasta threw out more crumbs. Edward watched her swoop down to catch another, but the bird escaped her grasp and the flock scattered again.

The pigeons were wary now, but Jocasta still managed to lure them close enough to catch another one before all the crumbs were gone. As she headed to the kitchen with them she threw a triumphant glance toward the window, and Edward wondered how the servant had known he and his sister were watching.

"I don't like that woman," Becky said, shrinking back.

"Neither do I," Edward agreed, but he knew he'd like the supper she would prepare that evening. The birds were small, but stewed with carrots and potatoes from the garden—and onions, too, of course—they would make a tasty meal. He tried to remember the last time he'd eaten his fill. He never actually left the table hungry, but he missed the feeling of satisfaction he'd always had after a meal at Riverview.

Edward frowned as he looked out over the garden that now took up most of the large backyard where he'd played croquet with his cousins on Sunday visits other summers. How did people who lived in the crowded part of the city with cramped back lots feed their families without a garden? What would Michael and his mother do this winter without a harvest of cabbages and root vegetables to see them through? Edward's frown deepened as he began to wonder if the autumn harvest of Aunt Charlotte's garden, added to the summer vegetables the women had canned, would be enough to feed all of *them* during the coming months. . . .

The next morning Edward was jolted from his sleep by regular reports of artillery fire. Remembering the hundred-gun salute fired on the Fourth of July, he wondered aloud, "Is it another Yankee holiday?"

BADOOM! BADOOM! BADOOM!

Duncan was struggling into his clothes. "Of course it's not a holiday," he snapped. "They're probably celebrating some victory. I'll go find out." He dashed from the room, and Edward heard him clatter down the stairs.

BADOOM! BADOOM! BADOOM!

Gritting his teeth, Edward got up and began to dress. Maybe the firing wouldn't sound so loud in the basement, he thought, and hurrying downstairs, he opened the door that led from the hall to the winter kitchen. He peered into the cool dimness below, and guided by the faint light that shone in through narrow windows high in the walls, he made his way down the steps.

Badoom! Badoom! Badoom!

Now the sound was slightly muffled. Edward sat on the bottom step with his hands over his ears and waited for the firing to stop. How did the men in the trenches stand it? When it was quiet at last, he drew a shaky breath and started back upstairs. He stepped into the hall at the same time his brother came in the front door with the newspaper.

"Hiding in the basement, were you?" Duncan sneered. "What's the matter, gun-shy?"

"I was looking for Jocasta," Edward lied.

"I'se right here, Marse Edward. What you want?"

Edward spun around to face Jocasta, noticing the triumphant glint in her eye. "It was nothing important," he muttered.

"If ever you needs me for somethin' 'portant, Marse Edward, you look for me outside in de *summer* kitchen," Jocasta said.

"What's going on here?" Aunt Charlotte asked as she came downstairs.

Duncan said, "It's Atlanta. The Yankees have taken the city. That's why they fired the salute—to rub it in and try to lower our morale. You know what this means, of course."

"No, Duncan, we're waiting for you to tell us," Mary Beth said from the foot of the steps.

Duncan didn't seem to notice the sarcasm in his cousin's voice. "Now that the North has won an important victory, there's a good chance Lincoln will be elected again in November," he announced.

"But everyone says that if he's elected, this war will go on and on!"

"You learn fast, cousin," Duncan said, and when Aunt

Charlotte gave him a sharp look, he quickly added, "I mean that as a compliment, Mary Beth."

Edward caught his cousin's eye and grinned. Duncan might be brave when it came to facing the enemy, but he was still a little afraid of his aunt.

Simon was proud that Hephestus, as the blacksmith called himself, hadn't needed to prompt him after the first day—not once in almost three weeks. By watching the color of the coals and the man's lightning-swift movements, he had quickly learned to anticipate when the smith would thrust his piece of metal into the forge.

Now! Simon leaned on the wooden pole that pumped the bellows, then watched Hephestus pull a glowing metal bar from the fire and raise his hammer. *Clang-a-lang-lang, Clang-a-lang-lang,* it sang as it fell, shaping the iron. *Clang-a-lang-lang!* Then came the hissing and spluttering when the smith plunged the metal into a water-filled barrel to cool.

Marveling that a white man could work so hard, Simon watched the cloud of steam rise. He gave the bellows a few quick pumps to make the graying coals blossom red, then grabbed the bucket and started off for water to refill the barrel.

Simon had gone only a few steps when he heard a high-pitched whistling. During the weeks he'd worked for the blacksmith, he'd become accustomed to the sounds of artillery and rifle fire in the distance, but this was different. Dropping the bucket, he began to run. Behind him, Simon heard a crash and the sound of splintering wood. He threw himself flat when he heard first a roar, then the resounding echo of an explosion.

Reliving the terrible day at the munitions wharf, Simon lay pressed to the earth, scarcely breathing, until he heard men's shouts. When he raised his head and looked back, he stared in disbelief at the inferno that had been the blacksmith shed. The blast had leveled the shed and twisted the huge bellows into an unrecognizable shape. The tinder-dry canopy of pine boughs had collapsed into the blaze, and sparks had ignited the canvas tops of two wagons waiting to be repaired. Teamsters were trying to pull a third wagon away from the fire, and the wheelwright had run from his shed to bend over an injured man. A man much too small to be Hephestus.

Hephestus! Simon's throat tightened. He closed his eyes and waited for a wave of nausea to pass, but his eyes flew open when he heard the whistling again and one of the teamsters yelled, "Now them Rebs are aimin' at the flames!"

The pitch changed as the whistling sound grew louder, and Simon flattened his body against the ground, terrified. The shell hit so close he was showered by the dirt that splashed up behind it, and when he opened his eyes, he saw that it had plowed a deep furrow through the sunbaked earth. If it had hit a few feet sooner—

Simon scrambled to his feet and ran. He pounded over the parched ground and leaped across ditches until he had no breath left. Exhausted, he sank to the ground and lay gasping until he slowly became aware of the familiar hardness of the field glasses against his body. He raised his head and glanced around. Where was he?

Simon sat up and shrugged his arm under the strap so that the field glasses hung around his neck instead of at his side. He raised them and scanned the area until he saw a cloud of dust that moved steadily to the northeast. "Cavalry patrol," he muttered. "Cavalry patrol headed back to City Point." He kept his glasses trained on the cloud, fixing in his mind the location of the road. The road that would lead him away from the danger of enemy shells and back to Riverview.

Now the firing in the distance sounded more like fireworks and popguns than weapons that could cause the destruction he'd just seen, but it still made Simon think of Hephestus. Hephestus, who had praised him for his hard work. Hephestus, who had been good to him.

"I'd of been killed, too, if I hadn't started off to get more water," Simon whispered. He'd have been killed, and no one would care. There wasn't anyone *to* care. Edward would have cared, Simon told himself, but then he remembered that Edward wouldn't have known.

His heart heavy, Simon hauled himself to his feet and set off once more toward City Point. He'd stay away from the wharf, he promised himself, and from the contraband camp, too. Right now he was too shaken to think about what he *would* do, but he'd manage.

"I'll stick with the Union army," he whispered. That's what Ambrose had said he should do—stick with the Union army. . . .

It was late by the time Simon passed the huge hospital complex the army had built in what had been one of Riverview's wheat fields. Most of the canvas-walled wards were dark, but a few of them glowed with lamplight, and he could see shadowy figures moving about inside.

In spite of his fatigue, Simon walked faster until he had left the hospital behind. He didn't want to be reminded of pain and suffering. Or death. This time last night, Hephestus was alive. "Don't think about it," Simon said, his voice loud in the darkness. Not thinking about it was the only way he knew to stop the ache deep in his chest.

When he finally came to the wagon park, Simon was amazed at how much larger it was than when he'd camped with Uncle Hap. His lagging steps quickened at the thought of the old man. Maybe—

With renewed energy, Simon made his way to the teamsters' camp, but though he walked up and down between their rows of shelter tents, he didn't see a familiar face. Most of the men sitting around the campfires ignored Simon, but a few looked at him suspiciously, and one of them called, "It pas' curfew, boy—what you doin' 'way from dat camp?"

Simon's heart beat faster. He had to find somewhere to sleep, somewhere the provost guards who patrolled the huge camp wouldn't find him. His mind turned to the acres of army wagons parked almost wheel to wheel. The guard wouldn't find him there.

Simon made his way between the rows of wagons until he figured he must be near the center of the lot before he climbed into one of the canvas-topped vehicles. He would be safe here. Gripping the strap of his field glasses with one hand, Simon cushioned his head on his arm and tried not to think about the whistling of artillery shells or the crackling flames that had destroyed the blacksmith shed. "Think about tomorrow," he whispered.

First thing tomorrow he'd get himself a blanket from the

Freedmen's Aid Society, and then he'd go to the bakery and help load trays of fresh-baked loaves into the cars of the army train that would take them to the men in the camps. That would earn him his daily bread. Maybe by tomorrow his stomach would have unknotted so he could eat.

SEPTEMBER 5, 1864

It was hard to believe there was a war going on, Simon thought as he stood watching the parade at City Point, but he'd heard that President Lincoln himself had set today aside to celebrate the fall of Atlanta a few days before.

Simon had no idea where Atlanta was, and he didn't much care. All he cared about was Petersburg, and it seemed no closer to falling than it had three months ago. His attention turned to the Negro regiment that was marching by, and he cheered so loudly that a group of teamsters turned to stare at him. After the Negro soldiers had all passed, Simon ducked back through the crowd of contrabands and headed for the field where the entertainment would take place.

A band was playing and flags flew everywhere. Caught up in the festive spirit, Simon decided that he was enjoying his freedom more today than he ever had before. He glanced at the wooden booths where lemonade and cakes were displayed for sale. Feeling in his pocket for the money he'd earned filling canteens with fresh water for the soldiers in the army prison yard, Simon smiled. Later, he'd buy himself some of that lemonade.

A tantalizing smell wafted toward him, and Simon shaded his eyes with his hand to look for its source. He grinned when he saw that whole pigs were being roasted over fires built in a long trench. Pairs of young Negro boys were turning the spits and laughing together, and as Simon watched them, his smile began to fade. He wished he had a friend—someone like Edward, only black.

Hoping to revive his good spirits, Simon joined a crowd cheering for a man trying to climb a greased pole, then wandered over to watch a relay race. He was thinking about buying a lemonade when he heard someone say, "Well, well, what have we here?"

Even before he saw the taunting expression on the soldier's face, Simon was afraid. He backed away, but a voice behind him said, "Not so fast! You haven't told my friend what you are." He pushed Simon forward until he was so close to the soldier who had spoken first that all he could see were the buttons on the man's uniform.

"Must be a sheep," the soldier said, rubbing his knuckles across Simon's bare head. "It's covered with wool. See?" He shoved Simon toward his companion, who gingerly felt Simon's short, nappy hair.

Simon forced himself to stand passively, hoping the men would tire of their sport if he didn't react. But the first soldier said, "A black sheep, perhaps. Or maybe a monkey. Let's see if it's a dancing monkey."

His friend grinned. "Good idea," he said, and he stomped his huge boot just in front of Simon's bare toes. The boy sprang back, and with a roar of laughter, the soldier stomped at him again.

"Dance, monkey, dance!" shouted the men who had quickly gathered in a circle around him to watch. One of them began to clap, and then the whole group was clapping, faster and faster, and the bullying soldier matched his stomps to their claps.

"Higher! Jump higher!" someone shouted, and they all began to chant, "HIGH-er! HIGH-er!" as they clapped.

Simon's heart pounded. He couldn't jump any higher! He was about to collapse from fear and exhaustion when a ruddy-faced man forced his way into the group and bawled, "Private Kelly!"

Simon's tormentor whirled around. "Yes, sir!" he said, saluting.

"You're a disgrace to your regiment! What do you have to say for yourself?"

"Just celebratin', sir. Just havin' a little fun."

The officer looked at him with disgust. "Well, have your fun with somebody your own size. Go on, now!" As Private Kelly slunk off in search of the companions who had melted into the crowd, the officer turned to Simon. "You'd better stay where you belong so something like this doesn't happen again," he said gruffly.

Still gasping for breath, Simon nodded. But where *did* he belong? White soldiers were everywhere he looked, and Simon was seized with fear. He didn't think he'd ever forget those huge, stomping boots. He'd have been crippled for life if one of them had landed on his bare foot, and then what would have become of him? "It's a good thing that officer came along when he did," Simon muttered as he skirted the edge of the field and headed for the wagon park.

After he had made his way to the vehicle where he'd spent the past few nights, Simon stretched out on its floor and rested his throbbing head on his blanket roll. It was hot and stuffy beneath the wagon's rounded cover, but it was safe. Simon listened to the faint sounds of band music and men's voices cheering, and he felt more alone than he'd ever felt before.

SEPTEMBER 17, 1864

Edward looked at the dragon he'd drawn and wished he had some paints to color it with. He'd make it blue, he thought, like the dark-skinned blue beast that had surged up the lane toward Riverview last May. Blue, like the frightful creature that was stretching its tentacles around Petersburg and spewing its fiery—

Shaking off the vivid mental images, Edward whispered, "Simon was right. I *do* scare myself." He bent over his paper and quickly began to sketch a knight who would slay the dragon, planning how he'd make the knight's banner the Confederate battle flag and then letter "CSA" on the knight's shield in Old English script. He was so intent on his work that he paid no attention to the doorbell's ring, but he slowly became aware of the sound of excited voices.

Curious, he stepped into the upstairs hall just as his cousin hurried up the stairs calling, "Edward! It's your papa!"

"Father!" Edward cried, and he ran downstairs to hurl himself into his father's arms. "You're safe!" Thin and worn-looking, but safe. Edward closed his eyes and breathed in the scent of horse and sweat and campfire smoke.

"Of course he's safe," Duncan said impatiently. "Father, did you know that Edward checks the casualty list every day to make sure your name isn't on it?"

"Not every day," Edward protested, glaring over his shoulder at his brother. "Maybe once or twice a week."

Father held him at arm's length and looked at him with disapproval. "I'm glad I didn't know that," he said. "Promise me you'll stop—it's enough to turn a fellow's luck."

"I promise," Edward said quickly. "I won't ever read those lists again." But what would he do instead when worry threatened to overpower him?

"We mustn't keep your father standing in the hall," Mother said, shepherding them into the sitting room. "Let's visit here while Jocasta cooks him a late breakfast."

The servant called them into the dining room a short time later, and Edward's eyes widened when he saw what she had prepared. He hadn't known there was any ham left.

"This is wonderful," Father exclaimed, looking from the thin slices of ham and the silver basket piled high with biscuits to the slices of tomato fresh from the garden and the bowl of peaches the women had canned. "Just the thing to make me forget a week in the saddle, most of it behind enemy lines."

"Behind enemy lines? Tell us about it, Father!" Duncan's voice was eager.

Father shrugged and said, "Not much to tell. We simply

rode all the way around the Union lines and brought out about twenty-five hundred head of their cattle." He grinned, adding, "Our army will feast tonight—and a good many more nights, too."

Duncan could hardly contain his glee. "But how did you manage to do that right under the Yankees' noses?"

Edward felt a tug on his sleeve and leaned toward Becky. "Father's telling about how the cavalry took the Yankees' cattle and herded them back here so General Lee's army can have beef to eat," he whispered.

"You mean they stole them?" Becky asked, her eyes wide with disbelief. "And Father helped?"

"It's all right, Becky. In wartime people are allowed to do things that are wrong when we're at peace," Edward whispered back.

"But do they have to?"

"Yes!" Edward hissed. "Now be quiet." He turned his attention to Father and saw that he had finished his meal and was tracing a map on the tablecloth with his finger. Duncan watched, listening intently, but Father's enthusiastic description of the cavalry's route made no sense at all to Edward. He saw Becky slip out of her chair and stand beside Father, saw him absently put an arm around her waist and draw her close as he talked with Duncan.

For a moment, Edward wished he were seven years old again. He glanced at Mother, wondering if she felt left out, too, and saw that her eyes never moved from her husband's face. She seemed satisfied simply to be in the same room with Father, Edward thought, but that wasn't enough for him. He felt cheated.

At last Father pushed his chair back from the table and

said, "Well, now you've had a firsthand account of the cattle raid, and I've had a fine breakfast. I'll have to ride hard to catch up with the others, but this was worth it."

"You're leaving? But you just got here," Mother cried.

"Can't you stay a little longer?" Becky pleaded.

But Father shook his head, and after a flurry of hugs and handshakes he was gone. It was a relief to know his father was safe, Edward thought, slowly climbing the stairs, but— He stepped aside so Jocasta could pass on her way down.

"Marse Duncan, he brave like his pa," she muttered as she brushed by him, "but I don' know 'bout dis one here."

Edward felt a rush of anger that started at his feet and swept upward, making his head swim. "Just a minute, Jocasta," he said, and when she stopped to look back at him, he asked, "Did you have something to say to me?"

She shook her turbaned head and said, "I ain't got nothin' to say to you, Marse Edward. Nothin' at all."

Edward watched her disappear down the hall. He was glad he'd confronted her, even though he didn't much like her response.

Edward gave a start when the clock struck the hour. In the excitement of Father's visit that morning, he'd almost forgotten he was supposed to meet Michael. He burst out of the front door just as Michael reached the gate.

"Want to go down to one of the prisons?" Michael asked when they met. "We ain't done that for a while."

Edward quickly agreed. Seeing the sad-faced men staring out the prison windows always made the enemy seem less of a threat, at least for a little while.

As the boys approached one of the converted factory

buildings where captured Yankees were held till they could be shipped off to prison camps, Edward saw the men crowded around the windows. "I'll bet those are prisoners from the cattle raid," he said, and he told his friend about the cavalry's daring feat, without mentioning his father's part in it. He didn't want to seem boastful, but even more, he didn't want to face Michael's surprise that Father's visit had been so short.

Walking toward the building, Michael held his hands to his face and bawled like an angry bull, and unable to resist, Edward began to moo loudly. A man at a downstairs window yelled something at them, and Michael hollered, "Too bad you won't get none of that Yankee beef our army's gonna feast on!"

One of the prisoners shouted back, "They'd better make it last, 'cause once we've taken all your railroads, they won't be getting anything else to eat. And neither will the rest of you Rebels in this cursed city."

Edward felt a stir of fear at the man's words, but he forced it down. He cupped his hands around his mouth and called back, "If we can rustle your cattle right out from under your noses, I guess we can keep our rail lines open." Even when the Yankees did cut a rail line, they couldn't keep the supplies from reaching Petersburg, Edward told himself. He'd seen the long strings of mule-drawn army wagons that met the trains and hauled supplies to the city, bypassing an enemy entrenchment on one of the railroads.

A prison guard limped toward them and said, "Go on home, boys. It's not decent to kick a man when he's down."

Edward was chagrined, but Michael said, "They deserve to be down. They're our enemies, ain't they?"

The elderly guard shook his head. "No, son, their government and our government are enemies, but those are just ordinary men who are serving their country. Serving what was *our* country until a few years ago, I might add. Now go on home and leave them be."

As they walked away, Edward barely heard Michael's grumbling. He was thinking about what the old man had called the prisoners. Were they really just ordinary men serving their country? Maybe so, Edward decided, but they were enemies just the same.

LATE SEPTEMBER

Edward was half disappointed, half relieved that he wouldn't be starting school the next week after all. It would have given him something to do, but he felt uneasy about trying to learn in a room full of other boys when he was used to working with a tutor.

As he walked home beside his mother, Edward tried to block out her tirade. First she had railed against the academy's headmaster, who had refused to let her pay his tuition with Confederate bills, and now she had started in on *him*.

". . . best school in the city. I've never been so embarrassed in my life. Are you listening to me, Edward?"

"I'm sorry you were embarrassed, Mother, but I couldn't let you barter food for my schooling. Didn't you hear Uncle Gilbert say that if the siege continues over the winter, people in the city will go hungry?"

"Poor people and refugees, perhaps," Mother retorted, "but certainly not people like us."

Edward wasn't so sure about that. He was proud that he'd spoken up and politely told the headmaster that they wouldn't be paying his school fees with potatoes or canned garden vegetables. Mother's anger was easier to face than the shame he would feel if she asked Aunt Charlotte to let her "spend" part of their harvest on his education. Hadn't his aunt done enough for them?

They walked without speaking again until they neared the house. "Look," Mother said, her anger apparently forgotten, "Charlotte's picking chrysanthemums."

Flowers on the table and his aunt's pretty china and glassware couldn't disguise the fact that their portions were getting smaller, Edward thought, wondering why Mother hadn't noticed that. But as he looked at Aunt Charlotte's golden bouquet, he could feel his spirits lift. . . .

It was past midnight when Edward woke to a clang of bells. Fire bells, he thought as he made his way to the window. How could Duncan sleep through such a racket? Edward pulled back the curtain and saw a reddish glare in the sky. The clanging grew louder, and he saw a fire wagon roll past, its horses running at full tilt. What was burning? Something over by the reservoir, Edward decided, his eyes on the blaze again.

And then he had a terrible thought. What if the Yankee shells had hit the waterworks? Without water to fight the fires, the whole city might burn to the ground, and then what would become of them? Edward could almost see tongues of flames licking at the porch steps and leaping up the pillars, could almost hear the fire crackle and feel its heat.

The sound of running footsteps drew his attention to the street below, and he felt a little better when he saw soldiers hurrying in the direction of the blaze. Officers billeted in the neighborhood were on their way to help. He hoped they'd be as good at fighting fires as they were at keeping the Yankees at bay.

While Edward watched, the lurid glow slowly began to fade, and he knew it wasn't the waterworks that had been afire. Shivering in the darkness, he went back to bed.

He lay there, wide awake, for what seemed like hours. His stomach grumbled, and he wondered what time it was—or rather, how long it would be until breakfast. He never used to think about food like this, to bide his time from one meal to the next as he did now. It wasn't that he was hungry so much as that he simply wanted to eat. Wanted to eat for the sheer pleasure of it rather than for the sake of staying alive, wanted to enjoy the sweet sensation of ice cream melting in his mouth.

As he listened to Duncan's measured breathing, Edward thought of life back at Riverview, where they'd always had all they wanted to eat. Back where if he woke in the night, instead of Duncan's breathing he'd hear Simon whisper, "Anything you need, Marse Edward?"

Well, he could find his own extra blanket or pour his own glass of water, without any help from Simon. It still bothered Edward that he had thought of the other boy as a friend when to Simon he had simply been a duty. Michael was a friend, because if Michael didn't want to spend time with him, he wouldn't keep coming around.

Sighing, Edward wished he enjoyed Michael's company as much as he had Simon's. He wondered if he would ever again trust anyone the way he'd trusted Simon—or if he even *should.* After all, he'd been wrong once . . . .

The next day, Edward felt tired and listless. He was nodding over one of Wesley's books when he heard Jocasta's sharp footsteps stop at the sitting room door.

"Miss Charlotte say fer me to ask if you can use dis," the servant said, holding out an ancient musket.

"Of course I can," Edward said, offended. Father had taught him to shoot years ago. Wide awake now, he looked at the old-fashioned weapon with interest.

"Take it, den. A flock of blackbird done fly over dis mornin', and dey be flyin' back 'fore long."

"Are you sure my aunt wants me to waste ammunition protecting the garden? There's not much left besides winter squash and root vegetables." He'd picked the last of the green beans for Aunt Charlotte the day before.

Jocasta looked at Edward with thinly masked disgust. "She don' want you to waste none of dat 'munition. She 'spect you to make every shot count so's we can have meat pie when Marse Gilbert come to visit dis evenin'."

When it dawned on Edward what the woman meant, he stood up and reached for the musket and the box of shot. Outside, he loaded the gun and then leaned against the back fence to wait. As the late afternoon shadows lengthened and the sunlight became thinner, Edward wiggled his toes and rubbed his chilled hands together, wondering if Jocasta could be playing another trick on him. He had almost decided he'd been fooled again when he heard the beating of wings, and the sky above him darkened.

Edward raised the gun to his shoulder and fired into the air. The weapon's recoil knocked him backward, and by the time he'd regained his balance, dead birds were raining down around him. He reloaded, braced himself, and fired into the flock again. Again he heard the *plop, plop, plop* of blackbirds hitting the ground around him. And still they came. By the time only a few stragglers remained in the air above him, Edward heard the reports of guns from the streets beyond. Rubbing his shoulder where the musket's stock had bruised it, he thought of the blackbird flocks that had darkened the skies over the plantation morning and evening for days as they gathered for their fall migration. He should be able to shoot birds all week.

Even though it would have been impossible to miss the thickly massed blackbirds, Edward felt a sense of satisfaction as he watched Jocasta gather them up. His uncle would be pleased when he sat down to a dinner of meat pies tonight. If only Father— Stop it, Edward told himself. Remember what Uncle Gilbert said.

When he closed his eyes, Edward could almost feel the weight of his uncle's hand on his shoulder and hear him saying, "You mustn't worry so about your father, my boy. He's a born horseman, and the cavalry's a lot more to his liking than running the plantation ever was. He's smart enough and lucky enough to come through this war without a scratch. And if he doesn't, well"—and here his uncle had hesitated— "he sees this war as the high point of his life, you know."

Now, when Edward began to wonder about his father's safety, he remembered his uncle's words. Knowing that Father saw fighting for the Confederacy as an adventure rather than a duty seemed to free Edward from his need to worry, but it left him feeling a little uneasy about himself. Duncan was like their father, but who was *he* like? His cousin Wesley, maybe.

As Edward walked slowly toward the house he wondered why he seemed to fit into his aunt's family so much better than into his own.

Edward looked up from his sketch pad the next evening when Mary Beth came into the parlor, followed by her mother and a beaming Becky. "Doesn't Mary Beth look beautiful?" Becky asked.

Mother looked up from her mending and said with satisfaction, "She certainly does. It makes all those hours of sewing worthwhile, doesn't it, Charlotte?"

Mary Beth blushed, and Edward thought she couldn't have looked any prettier in a brand-new dress than she did in the one the women had made from an old gown of Aunt Charlotte's.

The doorbell rang, and Mary Beth hurried back upstairs. A moment later, Jocasta ushered a young man into the room. Politely, he bowed and greeted the women, murmuring, "Miss Charlotte; Miss Emily." Then he bowed to Becky and shook hands with Edward and Duncan. Jocasta stood watching, and Edward wondered how she felt now that the soldier she'd chased out of the garden was a welcome guest.

From the door to the parlor a soft voice said, "Good evening, Corporal Renwick," and the soldier bowed low over Mary Beth's hand.

After the young couple left the house, Mother said, "I still can't believe you're letting your daughter go out with someone you barely know."

"You're in wartime Petersburg now, Emily, not back on the plantation."

"But you know nothing about this Corporal Renwick's family," Mother persisted.

Aunt Charlotte's voice shook as she said, "I know that there's an empty place at his family's table and that his mother lies awake at night wondering if her son is safe and well."

"They're only going to a lecture at the library, Mother," Edward said, willing her to drop the subject.

"I think Daniel's nice," Becky said, and when she saw her mother frown she added, "But he *wants* us to call him Daniel."

Mother said, "I'm not sure I approve of the familiarity of first names when—"

"Oh, for pity's sake, Emily!" Aunt Charlotte exploded. "If the boy wants the comfort of being called by his given name, what harm can that do?"

"Please don't be angry, Aunt Charlotte," Becky said, her voice trembling.

Aunt Charlotte drew the little girl toward her and said, "There now, dear, I didn't mean to frighten you." Over Becky's head she said, "I don't know what's come over me tonight, Emily."

"It's this terrible war," Mother said. "How much longer must we go on like this?"

Duncan, who had been engrossed in the Boston paper one of the new prisoners had given him, looked up and said, "It will probably be a very long time, now that things are going well for the Yankees in the Shenandoah Valley and farther south."

Wesley's regiment was in the Valley, Edward thought uneasily.

"But the Yankees aren't any closer to taking Petersburg," Mother said. "Why don't they give up and go fight somewhere else?"

"One of the prisoners told me the men on their line are as tired of this siege as we are, but they want to 'finish the job,' as he put it." Duncan's voice was bitter.

"Does that mean they want to keep on fighting?" Becky asked. "Aren't they afraid of getting killed?"

Duncan sounded resigned now. "There isn't a lot of fighting in the winter, Becky. The armies just dig in and wait for warm weather, so pretty soon the Yankees won't have to worry much about getting killed."

"Then our men won't have to worry about getting killed, either," Edward said with relief, thinking of his father and Uncle Gilbert. And young Corporal Renwick—Daniel—too.

"That's right," Duncan said sarcastically. "They'll only have to worry about starving. Freezing to death and starving."

Edward was stunned. He fought down images of Confederate soldiers freezing to death and starving while the well-supplied Yankee army waited.

"Poor Father! And poor Uncle Gilbert," Becky whispered.

"Your father and uncle won't starve as long as there's a

mouthful of food in this house," Aunt Charlotte assured her.

And as long as they can get home, Edward added silently. Father's only visit had been that brief one the day of the cattle raid, and they wouldn't be seeing much of Uncle Gilbert now that his unit was being moved farther from the city. Edward thought of how he would miss his uncle's visits, miss Uncle Gilbert's interest in his artwork, miss their talks.

Edward stared down at his half-finished drawing and decided he would finish it the next day when the sun pouring through the windows had warmed the sitting room. He rubbed his cold hands together and wished they could have a fire to take the chill off these autumn evenings instead of saving fuel for winter. He thought longingly of the days when fires burned brightly in every room of Riverview, of the luxury of dressing in front of the fire in his bedroom—the fire Simon built each morning. Edward sighed. He couldn't help wondering what had become of Simon.

OCTOBER, 1864

Simon stood by the well of an abandoned farmhouse west of the city and watched the men building new fortifications, extending the Union line. As he turned the crank to raise a bucket of water, he wondered fleetingly what had become of the people who lived on the farm before it became a battlefield.

When the creaking chain brought the water bucket to the edge of the well, Simon replaced it with an empty one, and his eyes wandered as he cranked to raise the second bucket. For as far as he could see in both directions, groups of enlisted men were digging trenches and piling up the dirt to form new earthworks while their officers shouted orders.

In the army, officers were the masters and everybody else was a slave, Simon thought as he hooked the water buckets onto the yoke. Or rather, he corrected himself, the officers were overseers and General Grant—or maybe even the president, for all he knew—was the master. Grunting with the effort, Simon raised the yoke to his shoulders and started toward the thirsty men.

He'd rather work here than on the wharf or the front line, Simon thought, but the best job of all had been the one he'd had when he left the wagon park to be water boy for the crews building the military railroad. How those men had worked, building trestles and laying track so trains could supply soldiers in the camps and trenches with everything they needed. He'd been sorry when the crews had finished their work.

Simon could feel the eyes of the dusty, sweating men measuring his progress, and he walked as fast as he could without spilling the water. He shifted the heavy yoke a little to ease its pressure on the sore it had rubbed on his left shoulder. Now that the days were cooler, this wasn't such a bad way to earn his keep, Simon thought.

He stopped so that a group of soldiers could drink, and as he waited, an open wagon pulled up. "Burial detail," the driver called cheerfully. Behind him, two privates were tossing down the bodies of men killed in battle the day before, spreading them along the slowly rising earthworks. Soldiers digging the trenches threw spadesful of dirt over the bodies, while Simon watched, horrified.

"What's the matter, boy? Ain't you never seen a dead Rebel before?" asked one of the workers. Simon shook his head and the man said, "Long as we got to bury 'em, might as well put 'em to use buildin' up our works, don't you think?"

Simon stumbled away, the man's jeering laughter following him. He was barely aware of the thirsty men who were gathering around him until he felt a hand on his arm and heard a voice ask, "You all right, son?" Simon raised his eyes to the concerned face of a black soldier, a large man who looked to be in his thirties. Not trusting his voice, Simon nodded. But when he heard the wagon approaching and the call "Burial detail," he shook his head.

The man's gaze was intense. "The body is only a shell," he said. Nodding toward the wagon, he added, "Those are empty cocoons left behind when the spirits soared away. Remember—"

But before he could finish, a white officer shouted, "Corporal Jackson! No shirking."

Simon headed toward the next group of thirsty soldiers. The yoke still rubbed his shoulder, but he hardly noticed. He was thinking about Corporal Jackson and what he had said. Somehow, he seemed different from the other soldiers. He even sounded different, almost like the tutor Edward and his brother had before the war. . . .

That evening, Simon walked up and down the rows of tents, looking for the corporal. When he saw him, he paused, and the man looked up from his meal and called, "You want some supper, water boy?" Simon nodded and headed toward the campfire. As he set down his sack and pulled out his tin plate the corporal asked, "You on your own?" Simon nodded again, and after glancing around the campfire circle the man said, "You can stay with us, if you want. I'm Gabriel, and these are Jake, Henry, and Julian."

"I'm Simon. I can polish your brass an' do whatever else you want." He bent over his plate so the men wouldn't see how glad he was to be joining them.

"Still hungry?" Gabriel asked. "There's more."

Simon nodded and held out his plate for another helping. For the first time since his brother was killed, he felt he might have found a place where he could belong. . . .

Later that evening Simon slipped away from the group that was singing around a bonfire at the far end of the camp and made his way back to Gabriel's site. He sank down onto one of the logs the men had placed around the campfire and stared into the coals. The sound of voices floating across the moonlit darkness made him think of all the nights he'd sung with Ambrose and his messmates. Simon sat brooding about his brother's death until the sound of footsteps caught his ear and he sensed that Gabriel had come to look for him.

"Aren't you going to sing with us, Simon?"

"Don't feel much like singin'," Simon said, but his spirits rose a little when Gabriel sat down opposite him. They listened together as the music swelled in a plaintive chorus and the voices sang, *". . . an' te-ell ol' Pha-ay-roah to let my people go."*

The sadness on Gabriel's face prompted Simon to ask, "You got family still in slavery? I'd figured you were from up north."

"I am. For as far back as anybody can remember, my ancestors have lived free in Philadelphia. But the slaves are my people, too, Simon. That's one reason I'm in this war."

"*One* reason?" Simon echoed. Wasn't freeing the slaves the only reason anybody needed?

Gabriel leaned forward and said, "I'm fighting for the free Negroes, too, Simon. Being free isn't enough—we want to be full citizens. To vote. Don't you see?" he asked earnestly. "If the men who run the country let us fight for the United States, how can they refuse to let us vote for its leaders?"

"I—I guess they can't." The intensity of Gabriel's voice unnerved Simon, and he stood up, saying, "I guess maybe I'll join in the singin' after all." He wasn't ready to think about voting.

Simon's boots crunched through the thick layer of frost as he headed for the sutler's tent, where sweets and other small luxuries were sold. A group of white soldiers pushed their way past him on their way out, and clutching the greenback Gabriel had given him, Simon went inside. He glanced around the spacious tent and saw that the only other customer was a young officer who stood looking at a magazine, his back to the door.

The sutler scowled at Simon and the boy quickly pushed his bill across the counter. "Please, suh," he asked, instinctively speaking the way he sensed the white man expected him to, "can I git five of dem Linkum badges?"

Reluctantly, the sutler counted out five campaign badges with Lincoln's picture and pocketed the bill. When Simon made no move to leave, the man growled, "Well, what are you waiting for, boy?"

"My change, suh." Simon had heard that the sutler

cheated Negro soldiers, if he waited on them at all, and now he knew it was true.

The man leaned so close Simon could see the coarse pores on his nose. "You sayin' I cheated you, boy?" he asked menacingly.

"No, suh! I'se jus' waitin' for my change." Only concern that Gabriel might think *he'd* kept the change prevented Simon from bolting out of the sutler's tent.

The man's face twisted with anger and he grabbed the front of Simon's coat and jerked him against the counter. "Why, you uppity little—"

But before he could finish, the officer spoke sharply. "Give the boy his change, Sully."

After a brief hesitation, the sutler released Simon and slammed his change onto the counter. Simon snatched it up and headed for the door at the same time the officer turned to leave. The boy raised his eyes to the man's face and saw that it was the young lieutenant—now a major—he'd worked for when the army took over Riverview. The major glanced at Simon, but his face showed no sign of recognition.

Simon wondered if that was because he was wearing the knit cap and too-large overcoat he'd gotten from the Freedmen's Aid Society, or if all "darkies" looked alike to the officer.

Outside the sutler's, Simon paused to pin one of the badges to his coat, remembering the day Ambrose had seen the president. A wave of sadness swept over him at the thought of his brother, and he muttered, "Stop feelin' sorry for yourself. Be glad you can camp with Gabriel and the others instead of bein' some white officer's darky."

LATE NOVEMBER, 1864

From the far side of the street, Edward watched the free Negro who owned the livery stable measure out corn for the army horses stabled there. Hunching his shoulders against the early morning chill, Edward waited while the liveryman and his two young sons curried the horses and saddled them for the officers who boarded nearby.

As soon as the horses were led away, Edward dashed across the street, pulling a small cloth bag from his pocket as he ran. He slipped between the fence rails and began to pick up the kernels of corn that had fallen to the ground when the horses were fed. He'd add them to his gleanings from earlier in the week, and Jocasta would char the kernels in the hearth and then grind them to make a coffee substitute. Sweetened with a little molasses, it made a tasty drink.

A few minutes later, Edward was on his way home, carrying a cup or so of corn. With the "coffee" Jocasta would make from it and the "tea" she brewed from blackberry leaves the girls had picked and dried last summer, they could have a hot drink whenever they pleased. Besides warming them, it seemed to fool their stomachs and keep them from feeling hungry between meals.

The whistling hiss of an approaching shell caught Edward's ear, and he ran a few yards and ducked into a narrow side street. He heard a crash and then a clatter of bricks and thought, They must be aiming at the church steeple again. As he stepped out of the alley, he remembered how frightened he'd been of the daily shelling when the siege began. "I guess you can get used to just about anything," he mused. . . .

That afternoon Edward looked up from his book when Mary Beth said wistfully, "What I wouldn't give to have a dress like that." She leaned over to show her mother a picture in the magazine she'd borrowed from her friend Agatha.

Duncan glanced at the picture and said, "Hoop skirts are downright unpatriotic at a time when cloth is in short supply."

"I don't think a bolt of pink silk would deprive the army of many uniforms, do you?" Mary Beth asked sweetly.

Duncan gave his cousin a disparaging look and said, "The time you spent making it would deprive the Confederacy of your work in rolling bandages or knitting socks for our men."

Distracted by the sound of the doorbell, Mary Beth said, "Oh, I hope that's—"

But before she could finish, Jocasta appeared and said disapprovingly, "Someone to see Marse Edward."

It must be Michael, Edward thought, his spirits rising as he hurried toward the door. When he saw his friend, Edward understood Jocasta's disapproval, for the boy looked even more disheveled than usual. And even thinner.

"I came to say good-bye," Michael said, refusing to step past the entryway. "We're leavin' here. Takin' the train to Danville in the mornin'."

Edward's spirits plummeted. "I—I'll miss you," he said. "A lot."

"Yeah." Michael shifted his weight from one foot to the other and nodded.

Not knowing what else to say, Edward held out his hand and stammered, "Well, um, good luck."

Awkwardly, the boys shook hands, and Edward noticed for the first time that the sleeves of Michael's jacket ended several inches above his wrists and that his bare hands were badly chapped. Impulsively, he said, "Wait here—I have to get something."

Moments later he was back with his mittens and knit cap. "A going-away present," he said, handing them to the other boy.

"Gosh, I ain't had a present since before the war," Michael said as he slipped on the mittens and pulled the cap down over his ears. "Thanks!"

Edward walked Michael to the gate, wishing he could think of something to say, something more than just good-bye.

"Meetin' you was the one good thing that happened to me the whole time we was in Petersburg," Michael said, his words coming in a rush. And then he was gone.

Edward watched until his friend turned the corner, then slowly walked back to the house. Tonight he would draw Michael, he decided, draw him the way he looked just now—trudging away with one worn shoe sole flapping and the going-away-present cap on his bowed head.

"Drawing him will help me get used to the idea that he's gone," Edward whispered. Guiltily, he realized that he had taken the other boy for granted, that he'd just assumed Michael would always be stopping by the house and saying, "Hey, you want to do somethin' this afternoon?"

All eyes turned toward Edward when he came into the

sitting room, and he explained, "It was Michael, coming to say good-bye. He and his mother are leaving for Danville tomorrow."

"Good riddance. He was a most unsuitable boy," Mother said, "not at all the kind of person you'd have had for a friend back at Riverview."

"Back at Riverview, Edward didn't need a friend, 'cause he had Simon," Becky said.

Edward stared at the floor. Back at Riverview he'd thought Simon *was* his friend, but friends don't leave without saying good-bye. Even an "unsuitable" boy like Michael knew that. And Michael had said a better good-bye than *he* had, too.

"Why is it so quiet today?" Becky asked, breaking into Edward's thoughts, and he was suddenly aware that there had been little shelling and he hadn't heard the rattle of rifle fire for hours.

"It's a day of thanksgiving for the Yankees," Mary Beth said. "That's why I thought it might be Daniel at the door—Corporal Renwick, that is. He said our boys have been told to hold their fire while the Yankees celebrate their holiday," she added.

Duncan looked up from the paper. "Their whole army will be feasting on turkey today, while our men will go hungry."

"Well, none of our men who come here today will go hungry," Aunt Charlotte said. "We may not have turkey, but we have sweet potatoes, and Jocasta's making meat pies using the blackbirds we canned." She looked up from her mending to smile at Edward.

"I don't think we should celebrate the enemy's holiday," Duncan protested.

Aunt Charlotte said sharply, "We're not. We're celebrating having our soldiers at home with us on a day the guns are quiet."

It made no sense at all, Edward thought. Our army holds its fire while the Yankees have their turkey dinner, and the Yankees stop shelling the city every Sunday morning so people won't be afraid to go to church. And Duncan, probably the most patriotic Confederate in all of Petersburg, talks politics with the Yankee prisoners just like he would with anyone else.

It was more than Edward could understand.

The next day, the doorbell rang just as the family was sitting down to supper. Edward had been breathing in the tantalizing aroma of Jocasta's stew all afternoon, hungrily anticipating suppertime, and now he waited impatiently for the servant to return. It was about time, he thought when she came back down the stairs to the winter kitchen, followed by Daniel Renwick.

"Daniel!" cried Mary Beth. "It's so good to see you!"

"Set another place at the table, Jocasta," Aunt Charlotte said, "then take the stew back and warm it up."

The young soldier blushed and stammered, "I—I didn't know this was your suppertime, or I wouldn't have—"

"Nonsense! We're happy to see you anytime you can get away from the line," Aunt Charlotte said, smiling.

"We eat early because we only have two meals a day now," Mother said peevishly, "and we spend most of our time here in this kitchen, because fuel is too scarce to have another fire."

Edward was embarrassed. What must Daniel think of Mother, complaining like that? Aunt Charlotte and Mary Beth never complained. Even Becky didn't.

Jocasta brought the tureen back to the table, and when she removed the lid, Edward saw there was more stew than there had been before. Aunt Charlotte had really been telling Jocasta to add water so it would serve an extra person, he realized, and somehow Jocasta had known what she meant.

The woman ladled the stew into bowls, and after his first spoonful Daniel exclaimed, "This is delicious! I thought the Yankees were the only ones with beef. We haven't had any since that raid on their cattle pens."

"Jocasta's a fine cook," Aunt Charlotte said. "She makes do in spite of shortages."

Glancing up at his aunt's servant, who was grinding kernels of charred corn in the coffee mill for their after-dinner drink, Edward saw a strange expression cross her face. And as he chewed a succulent chunk of meat, he began to wonder how she had managed to buy beef.

Edward spooned up his stew and watched Jocasta fill Daniel's bowl a second time, thinking that she'd never offered *him* another helping of anything. Jocasta's attitude toward the young soldier certainly had changed, Edward mused. Was it because he was Mary Beth's beau now? Or could there be some other reason?

When dinner was over and the chairs were drawn close to the fire, Edward found himself watching Jocasta. He sensed that she was listening, although her back was to them as she scoured her wooden chopping block. She certainly seemed interested in what Daniel was saying, Edward thought. Come to think of it, she was always interested in anything Uncle Gilbert had to say, too.

Staring into the fire now, Edward blocked out the conversation so that he could concentrate on the idea forming in his mind. If what he thought was true, it would explain why Jocasta hovered about when the soldiers were there—and why they ate as well as they did when so many in the city were hungry. Maybe Jocasta was trading information to the Yankees for food—including Yankee beef. *Maybe Jocasta was a spy!*

Edward had almost decided to speak to Aunt Charlotte about his suspicions when he remembered the strong bond between his aunt and her servant. He'd seen them working companionably, side by side—something quite different from his mother's relationship with even her favorite Negroes at Riverview. He needed proof before he said anything. Well, he'd get that proof, and once he had it, his aunt would have to accept the truth about her servant.

Edward gave a guilty start when he looked up and saw Jocasta at the sitting room door. Did she know he had followed her all morning? First he'd trailed her to the back door of a small house on the far side of town and watched through a knothole in the fence while she handed a fresh-baked loaf of bread to the frail old woman who answered her knock. And later, he'd slipped along behind her when she went to Confederate headquarters to deliver a bundle of socks the women had knitted for the men in the trenches.

Just because she hadn't done anything suspicious yet didn't mean she wasn't spying for the Yankees, Edward thought, watching her come in and stand respectfully in front of his aunt.

"What is it, Jocasta?" Aunt Charlotte asked.

"Dat las' barrel of cornmeal Miss Emily brung is 'most use up, Miss Charlotte."

"Already? Shouldn't it have lasted longer than this?" Edward wondered aloud.

Jocasta sent a withering look in his direction. "Not wid feedin' every soldier dat come to de door an' sendin' meal back to camp wid Marse Dan—"

"That will be enough, Jocasta," Aunt Charlotte said sternly. Edward watched her cross the room to the mahogany desk and take a coin from a drawer. She handed it to the servant and said, "Go to Mr. Endicott's store and ask the price of a barrel of flour. When he tells you, say, 'Miss Charlotte wondered if you would take this for it instead,' and hand him the coin."

Jocasta nodded and slipped it inside her glove. After the door had shut behind her, Mother said, "I can't believe you still have gold pieces, Charlotte. We were all supposed to exchange our United States money for Confederate bills."

"I know we were," Aunt Charlotte said, "but aren't you glad I didn't?"

Without looking up from her knitting, Mother said, "I don't mean to criticize, but it seems so—well, so unpatriotic."

Edward could hardly believe his ears. Had Mother forgotten how the headmaster at the academy refused to take her Confederate currency? She should be glad her sister hadn't exchanged gold for worthless paper!

Aunt Charlotte said tartly, "You and the men can worry about patriotism if you wish, Emily, but I'm going to worry about feeding my family. And yours."

Mother's face flamed red, and she stood up so quickly her ball of yarn rolled across the rug. "I'm very sorry to have to burden you with feeding my family, Charlotte," she said.

"Sit down, Emily." Aunt Charlotte bit off a thread and smoothed a seam of the dress she was making Becky from an old skirt of Mary Beth's. "This is no time for either one of us to be so touchy." She waited until Becky had retrieved the yarn and Mother had settled back in her chair again, an injured look on her face. "I simply meant that I don't look at things the same way our government officials in Richmond do."

Aunt Charlotte paused to thread her needle. "When Gilbert left to fight for the South," she went on, "he gave me the week's receipts from his business and withdrew his savings from the bank for me to exchange for Confederate bills as soon as they were available here."

"But you held back all the gold pieces." Mother's tone was disapproving.

Aunt Charlotte nodded. "And all the banknotes drawn in northern states, too."

"You mean you disobeyed Father?" Mary Beth asked.

Aunt Charlotte gave her a sharp look. "You can say that if you wish, or you can say that I used my own judgment."

"I'm glad you did," Mary Beth said quickly. "I was just a little surprised."

"We live in surprising times," Aunt Charlotte replied. "Now come here, Becky, and let's see if this dress is long enough."

Edward watched the little girl stroke the rose-colored wool of the dress her aunt held up to her, and he wondered what would have become of them all if Aunt Charlotte hadn't been there to take them in.

Edward slid the heavy volume from the bookshelf in his uncle's library and opened it to the back. His hand shook a little as he carefully sliced out the blank pages at the very end, just before the cover. He never would have thought to do that if he hadn't watched his cousin write a letter to her brother on a sheet of onionskin that had covered a map in one of her old schoolbooks.

With every wall of Uncle Gilbert's library covered by floor-to-ceiling shelves tightly packed with books, he would have an almost endless supply of drawing paper, Edward thought. The war would be over long before he could possibly cut out all the blank pages.

" 'We live in surprising times,' " he muttered, repeating the words his aunt had used the day before, trying to ease the guilt he felt at tampering with his uncle's books. " 'We live in surprising times,' " he said again. "Desperate times, even." He wouldn't be doing this if he weren't desperate, Edward told himself. He *had* to draw.

Returning the book to the shelf, he replaced the chair he'd stood on and brushed off its leather seat, and when he looked up, Jocasta was standing in the doorway watching him.

"Hmph," she said as though talking to herself while she ran the feather duster along the shelves nearest the door. "'Least he won't be tearin' off de wallpaper back of de wardrobe in Marse Wesley's room an' drawin' on dat no more."

Edward's face burned. He'd only torn off one small piece, and it was loose anyway. He stalked from the room, ashamed at being found out but confident that Jocasta wouldn't tell anyone what he'd done. She'd mutter something that only he could hear, instead. Just wait. Sooner or later, Jocasta would be careless, and he'd have his proof that she was a spy.

Upstairs, Edward stashed his newfound paper supply under the rug, keeping out one sheet to draw on. A figure began to appear, and he paused to give it a critical look. "That's not how she stands," he muttered. Erasing here and there and changing a line or two made all the difference. He'd captured her defiant stance, head held high and one foot a little ahead of the other—something he had never consciously noticed—but something was wrong. It was the arms. Jocasta never stood with her arms at her sides.

Edward erased again and carefully blew away the tiny shreds of rubber. Then he sketched the left arm bent so the knuckles of the hand rested on her hip. That was more like it. But what about the right arm? He bent over the paper again, working until he was satisfied with the slightly raised, outstretched arm and the hand holding a feather duster.

The figure's stance was slightly menacing, exactly as he'd

imagined it, but the face wasn't Jocasta's. It didn't show the challenging thrust of her chin or the thinly veiled contempt in her eyes. He would have to try again, Edward decided, reaching for his eraser.

When he held up the paper and studied the finished drawing at last, a smile spread across his face. Not only was it the best work he had ever done—*it was Jocasta!* And now that he'd captured her on paper, she would never again be able to make him feel foolish and incompetent. Still smiling, Edward opened the bottom drawer of the bureau and carefully added the picture to the stack of drawings he kept underneath the nightshirt Wesley had left behind.

LATE NOVEMBER-EARLY DECEMBER, 1864

Simon breathed deeply, savoring the crispness of the November day and the tang of wood smoke that hung over the camp. Everywhere he looked, men were busy building their winter quarters—log huts roofed with layers of tent canvas stretched across a ridge pole. At least the heavy white material would let some daylight through, Simon thought as he watched Gabriel and Julian nail it to the top log of the wall.

He was thinking that the cabins in the slave quarters at Riverview had been far better, when Gabriel spoke. "This will seem like a palace after we come out of those bombproofs on the front line," he said as he stepped back to admire their work.

"I guess this means the generals figure the war's gonna

last all winter," Simon said, sensing that Gabriel expected a response.

Gabriel rested a hand on Simon's shoulder. "Sometimes it seems like it's going to last forever, but it won't."

It had already lasted so long he could hardly remember life at the Great House, Simon thought.

"Dem Rebel gonna starve long 'fore forever," Julian said confidently.

"Dem slavers deserve t' starve," Jake said, lapsing into a coughing spell.

Edward didn't deserve to starve, Simon thought, alarmed. He hoped Julian and Jake meant the Rebel soldiers and not the people in the city. . . .

That night as they all sat around the fire in the hut, Gabriel took out his harmonica and began to play. Silently, Simon repeated the words to the tune. He didn't remember them all, but he knew how it ended: "Be it ever so humble, there's no place like home."

Simon looked from the crudely built table to the shelflike bunks he had covered with thick layers of straw. He saw the haversacks and clothing hanging neatly from pegs Gabriel had driven between logs in the wall. This was a home, he realized. Not one like the Great House, but then that had been Edward's home. This one was *his.* He'd even helped build it, mixing mud and daubing it between the logs to keep out the wind and rain.

As the last strains of the song died away, Gabriel looked at Jake and frowned. Simon followed his gaze and saw that in spite of being near the fire, Jake was shivering. In the sudden quiet, the rasping of his breath was loud, and Simon hoped it wouldn't keep him awake the way the man's coughing sometimes did.

"Play something else, Gabriel," Simon said, hating the way Jake's labored breathing seemed to fill the hut. "Play something lively," he added. At first, he thought Gabriel hadn't heard him, but finally, with his worried eyes still on Jake, Gabriel brought the harmonica to his lips and began another song.

Simon stood with Gabriel outside the unpainted frame building that housed the provost marshal's office. He stamped his feet to keep warm while the line of soldiers waiting for passes snaked toward the door. Suddenly he felt himself shouldered aside, and a white soldier took his place.

Almost before Simon regained his balance he heard Gabriel say, "The line forms at the rear, soldier."

The white man turned to see who had spoken, and his obvious surprise changed to anger when he saw that a Negro had challenged him. But Gabriel didn't give him a chance to reply. "The end of the line is back there, private," he said, emphasizing "private."

The soldier's mouth tightened into a slit when he saw the two chevrons on Gabriel's sleeve. He stepped out of line, but instead of taking his place at the end he stormed off, cursing.

Simon was amazed. He had never thought he'd hear a Negro tell a white person what to do! Did those two small V-shaped stripes on Gabriel's uniform make that much difference? Simon saw looks of displeasure on the white faces around him and heard some angry muttering, but Gabriel didn't seem to notice.

Finally they were inside the building, and after another quarter hour they reached a desk where an officer sat surrounded by stacks of paper. "Yes?" he said without looking up.

"We need passes to give us leave to visit a friend in the hospital at City Point," Gabriel said.

The officer bent over his pad, scrawled a few words, and tore off two pages. "Next!" he called as he held out the passes.

Outside again, Simon looked at the hours scribbled on the paper, and his heart fell. "He hardly gave us enough time just to walk there and back!"

"We'll ride the train," Gabriel said, heading for the wooden platform that served as the camp's station. It wasn't long before an engine steamed up. Gabriel opened the door of a passenger car, and when Simon climbed in he was surprised to see tiers of narrow cots instead of seats.

"This is a hospital car," a medic said sharply, looking up from his patient.

Gabriel shut the door behind them and motioned Simon to the far end of the car. "That's fine," he said. "We're headed for the hospital, and we don't mind standing."

The train jerked forward, and Simon grabbed one of the wooden posts that supported the cots. He fought down the sense of panic he felt at being surrounded by suffering men and wished he'd never agreed to visit Jake. Staring at the floor, Simon kept his mind blank until he felt a terrible vibration and heard the screech of metal grating against metal. The train swayed and then began to slow, and as soon as it ground to a stop, he headed for the door.

When he stepped out onto the wooden platform, Simon stood and stared. This place must be almost as big as Petersburg! The canvas wards he remembered had been replaced by rows of frame buildings that lined wide graveled streets as far as he could see.

"So this is the hospital," Gabriel said as stretcher bearers brushed past on their way to unload the patients. "I'd heard it was large, but—" He tipped his cap to a woman pushing a cart loaded with clean bed linens. "Can you tell me how I can find a patient who was brought here two days ago?" he asked.

"De colored soldier, dere hospital be at de end of dat street," she said, pointing the way.

Simon followed Gabriel until they reached a gate with a sign that read UNITED STATES COLORED HOSPITAL. Beyond the gate stood more long frame buildings, and a sign on the first one said HEADQUARTERS. They went inside and waited for a middle-aged woman to look up from her desk. "We've come to visit Private Jake Jefferson, ma'am," Gabriel said.

The woman ran her finger down a list of names, muttering, "Jefferson . . . Jefferson." Her finger stopped, and she looked up at them. "I'm sorry," she said, "but Private Jefferson was buried yesterday. With full military honors," she added.

Buried? After escaping Rebel shells and bullets for over a year, Jake had *died?* Through a haze of confusion, Simon heard Gabriel say, "Then we'd like to visit his grave, ma'am," and he felt a chill in spite of the woodstove that heated the building.

Guiltily, Simon remembered how glad he'd been to see Jake taken to the field hospital, how he'd hated listening to Jake's constant cough, hated being kept awake by the rasp of his breathing. But he hadn't wanted him to die! How *could* Jake have died? Gabriel had said it was a good sign when Jake was brought to the main hospital, because the doctors moved only the men they thought would live. How could Gabriel have been wrong about something so important?

The woman unrolled a large chart and spread it open on the desk. "Here it is," she said at last. "I can tell you how to find your friend's resting place."

Simon's mouth felt dry. Reluctantly, he followed Gabriel to the section of the cemetery set aside for Negroes, staying close behind him while he counted the parallel rows of graves. At last Gabriel bent to check the name printed on a wooden cross stuck into a mound of earth. "Jacob Jefferson," he said quietly.

Jacob? It sounded like a stranger's name to Simon. He looked at the clods, trying not to think about what lay beneath them, but Gabriel took off his hat and faced the crude marker.

"Jake," he said, "Simon and I have come here because you were our friend. We'll miss you around our fire at night, but we know you have another resting place now, and that your spirit is free." Kneeling, Gabriel began to pray.

Simon stared at the mound of earth and told himself he shouldn't have minded Jake's coughing. He should have tried to help him sit up so that he could breathe more easily. Why had he felt as though his arms were tied to his sides? Simon remembered how Gabriel, his eyes filled with concern, would coax Jake to take a spoonful of porridge. *How dare Jake die?*

When Gabriel stood up, Simon said bitterly, "Jake doesn't know we came here. He couldn't hear a word you said."

"But you and I know we came," Gabriel said. "And I needed to say what I did. To say good-bye."

As he followed Gabriel back between the rows of white markers, Simon burst out, "I hate good-byes."

"So do I," Gabriel agreed, "but we'll both have our share of them before this war's over."

At the edge of the cemetery, Gabriel paused to look back across the rows of graves, but Simon pushed past him. He hurried by a man whose empty sleeve was pinned to the front of his coat, then shrank back against a wall as two men carrying a stretcher came toward him. His eyes followed the stretcher bearers as they went into a long, low building. He squinted to read the sign on the door: DEAD HOUSE.

Jamming his hands in his coat pockets, Simon headed for the platform where the military train would stop. He would never come to this terrible place again. Never!

That night, Simon polished the men's boots and tried not to think of why there were three pairs now instead of four. The fire in the hut's fireplace snapped and hissed, and Henry brushed away a spark that landed on his sleeve.

"President Lincoln says the Union will fight until the Rebels give up," Gabriel said, raising his eyes from the newspaper he was reading. "These are his very words: 'We have more men now than we had when the war began. . . . We are gaining strength, and may, if need be, maintain the contest indefinitely.'"

Indefinitely? Simon's hands paused in their work. Wasn't that the same as forever?

"What he sayin', Gabe?" asked Julian.

Gabriel folded the paper carefully before he answered. "He's saying that the Union is strong enough to fight until the Rebels are beaten, no matter how long it takes."

In the silence that followed Gabriel's words, Simon wondered how long that would be. And then, for the first time, he wondered what would become of him when the war was over. Forcing that question from his mind, he began to buff Henry's boot. The important thing was for the North to win the war so all the slaves would be free. He'd get along fine, no matter when that happened.

"How long you think it gonna take us to beat dem Rebel?" Julian asked.

Gabriel stared into the fire. "I don't know," he said at last, "but I'm in this war till it's finished. If it doesn't finish me first."

Gabriel's words hit Simon with the force of a blow. Would the war finish Gabriel? Would he lose him the way he'd lost everyone else he'd ever cared about? Silently, Simon repeated the names of the people who were lost to him: Mama, Poppa, Ambrose. And Edward, who had been the closest of all even though he was his master.

Simon lined up the boots he had polished, and then he added Hephestus and Jake to his list. They hadn't been as important to him as the others, but their deaths had shaken him. Shivering, he put another log on the fire and sank back onto his stool. His eyes moved from Julian, dozing with his head drooping, to Henry, intent on the piece of wood he was carving, and came to rest on Gabriel.

Gabriel sat staring into the fire as though he could read his future in the flames, and unsettled by the sadness of the man's face, Simon said, "Play us a tune, Gabriel."

After what seemed like a long time, Gabriel reached for his harmonica, and Simon settled back to listen.

Simon had heard of the sunken roads and walkways that allowed men and sometimes even supply wagons to move safely between the forts and trenches near the front, and now he was seeing them for himself. He had been almost glad to hear that Gabriel's unit was being sent to garrison one of the forts—now his eyes wouldn't be drawn to Jake's empty bunk a dozen times a day.

But as he walked through the drizzle, following Gabriel and the others along the sunken way, Simon's heart pounded. He had never been this close to the fighting before, and he half wished he could go back to the hut. He breathed deeply and reminded himself that no one else seemed concerned.

Once inside the fort, Simon looked around with interest. Along the base of the high, earthen walls ran a narrow raised step where riflemen stood. A short distance from the wall, squat-looking mortars aimed their wide barrels upward, ready to lob shells high in the air. Simon's skin crawled at the thought that the Rebels had mortars, too, and a Rebel shell could fall right where he stood.

He turned quickly toward the crude shelters that honeycombed the interior of the fort, dug into the earth like animal burrows. Those must be the bombproofs where the men stayed when they weren't on duty, Simon thought, staring. He saw Gabriel disappear into one of the cavelike structures and hurried after him. Inside, Julian was already building a fire, and soon the smell of wet wool mingled with the smoke and the dank scent of earth.

Gabriel began to play his harmonica, and Simon had just started to relax when crumbs of dirt showered down between the logs overhead. He felt a surge of panic, and his chest constricted the way it had when the clods of earth rained down on him as he lay on the wharf below the bluff the day the munitions barge exploded.

"Are you all right?" Gabriel asked, stopping mid-tune.

The weight of Gabriel's hand on his arm calmed Simon. "Do these things ever fall in on people?" he asked, squinting up at the low ceiling.

"Not that I've heard of," Gabriel said. "Not even when a shell hits. With a couple feet of earth piled over that log ceiling, this bombproof ought to live up to its name."

Henry added, "Long as you in here, you fine. It when you on watch dat you git kilt by dem mortar shell."

Simon shuddered. Now he understood why Gabriel had said the hut would seem like a palace when they came out of the bombproof.

MID-DECEMBER, 1864

"Is something wrong, Edward?" Aunt Charlotte asked. "Every time I've looked up, you've been staring at me."

His face reddening with embarrassment, Edward mumbled an apology and excused himself from the table. Upstairs, in the room he shared with Duncan, he set to work on the half-finished drawing of his aunt. He had almost managed to capture her expression of stern kindness when his brother came in.

Shaking his head in disbelief, Duncan exclaimed, "I don't understand you, Edward. The world's falling apart around us, and you're sitting up here in the cold drawing pictures." He took his coat from the wardrobe and looked at it critically.

"At least I'll have something to give for Christmas presents," Edward said.

"You might be able to get away with that for Mother," Duncan said, shrugging into the coat, "but I can't imagine why anyone else would want one of your amateurish sketches."

Edward stared after Duncan as his brother left the room. Amateurish sketches? He looked down at his drawing, and dissatisfied now with what he saw, he crumpled the paper into a ball and threw it on the floor. He was about to reach for a book he'd left on the bureau when Jocasta came in with her feather duster.

Watching her in the mirror, Edward saw her stoop to

pick up the crumpled paper and put it in her apron pocket. As he struggled to decide whether to ask her for it, their eyes met in the glass and a look of understanding crossed Jocasta's face. She took the drawing from her pocket and tucked the feather duster under her arm while she tried to smooth away the creases. Edward's hands clenched into fists as he watched her study it, tipping her head this way and that. "Ain't near as good as de one he done of me," she said under her breath.

The doorbell rang, and Jocasta crumpled the drawing and dropped it into her pocket as she left the room. Edward made a dive for the bottom drawer of the bureau. The picture of Jocasta was still in the stack under Wesley's nightshirt, but it had been turned upside down. She'd meant for him to know she'd seen it! Filled with helpless anger, Edward shut the drawer and went to the wardrobe for his coat. He had to get away from that woman!

But he forgot his anger when he reached the foot of the steps and saw the servant standing at the front door, her body rigid and her eyes full of dread. She thrust something at him—a letter addressed to his aunt and uncle. The name of a lieutenant in Wesley's unit was written on the flap, and Edward suddenly felt as though his heart was pumping ice water through his veins.

Edward looked up as Mary Beth and Becky burst into the house with their arms full of holly, and he saw the color drain from his cousin's face as she looked from Jocasta to the letter in his hand. Dropping the holly, Mary Beth snatched the envelope from him and broke the seal.

"Wesley," she whispered. The paper fell to the floor as

she ran upstairs, weeping and calling out her brother's name.

Jocasta wailed loudly and buried her face in her apron. As she stumbled away, Becky turned to Edward and whispered, "Is Wesley *dead?*"

Stalling for time to compose himself, Edward picked up the letter. He stared at the words— ". . . regret . . . fierce fighting . . . outnumbered . . . my deepest sympathy. . ."— till they began to make sense. "Killed almost a month ago," he said at last.

"But I *loved* Wesley!" Becky wailed. "I *loved* him!"

Numbly, Edward watched her collapse onto the bottom step, sobbing. He stood there helplessly, wondering what he should do, until to his great relief Mary Beth ran down the stairs, eyes red and hair disheveled, and drew the little girl into her arms.

Edward was wishing he could slip past them and escape to his room when Jocasta swept by, still weeping, wrapped in her shawl. "Where are you going?" he asked, surprised.

"To fetch poor Miss Charlotte," Jocasta sobbed.

"I'll go for her," Edward said quickly, seizing the opportunity to flee the sorrow-filled house. He blinked back tears and trudged toward the church where the women met to sew clothing for the soldiers in the trenches.

His steps slowed as he neared the building, and he wished he'd let Jocasta go after all. How was he going to tell his aunt? While he stood uncertainly by the side entrance of the church, two women carrying sewing baskets came toward him, and he opened the door for them. The older woman looked at him sympathetically and asked,

"Would you like me to tell your mama that you're here?"

Relief washed over him and he said, "Yes, please. My mother is Emily Slocumb." He'd tell Mother, and she could tell Aunt Charlotte.

It seemed only a moment before Mother was at the door, her face pale. "Is it your father?" she asked, gripping his arm in a grasp that made Edward wince.

He shook his head. "Wesley." It was hard to make his lips form the name.

Mother covered her face with her hands and Edward could barely hear her muffled words—first, "Thank God!" and then, "Poor Charlotte " Edward opened the door for her when she turned to go back inside, then jammed his hands in his pockets and started home, thinking about his cousin. Wesley had always been good to him—and to Becky.

What was it his cousin had said when Becky asked why he had to go and fight? Edward searched his mind until he thought he had the exact words: *"It's the law, Becky, but I'd have to do what's expected of me even if it weren't. I'm a Virginian, and an enemy army has invaded Virginia."* So instead of going to the university, Wesley had gone off to war.

Edward realized with a jolt that he wouldn't have felt nearly so sorry if it had been Duncan who was killed, since Duncan *wanted* to fight the Yankees. Duncan! Edward turned toward the prison, telling himself that his brother should know about Wesley before he came home to a grieving household. But deep down, he knew it was an excuse to delay going home, to avoid seeing his aunt weep.

As he approached the prison, Edward saw his brother

marching back and forth in front of the door, a rifle on his shoulder. Glad that he wouldn't have to go inside the building, Edward called, "Hey, Duncan!"

"Don't you know better than to come here when I'm on duty?" Duncan demanded when he saw his brother hurrying toward him.

"Wesley's dead."

"Dead! How?"

Trust Duncan to ask that, Edward thought. "Killed in a skirmish last month."

"Poor old Wesley. I might have known it would be a skirmish and not a real battle." Duncan looked into the distance. "Maybe Gettysburg. No, First Manassas," he said. "That was a victory. A rout, even. Now *that* would have been a battle to die in."

Edward felt such a wave of disgust that he turned away without a word. He walked toward home, hands in his pockets, head bowed, wondering if Wesley had suffered, wondering if he had been afraid. *He* would have been afraid, Edward thought. He could almost see himself dressed in Confederate gray, marching in a long column of men along a dusty road, could almost hear the shots ring out unexpectedly. His pulse raced, just as though he were really there, and he concentrated on breathing deeply to calm himself.

Would he have been too terrified to take cover and fire back at the enemy? So terrified he couldn't move? The lieutenant who wrote the letter about Wesley said that he'd fought bravely, that he was a son to be proud of. But what about *him?* If the war lasted until *he* was seventeen, would he make Mother and Father proud of him—or would he shame them?

Once when he had admitted to Uncle Gilbert that he was sure he'd never be brave like Father and Duncan, his uncle had told him not to worry, that when he needed courage, he would find it. Edward hoped that was true.

His steps began to lag as he approached the house and saw the black crepe ribbon on the door, the sign of a house of mourning. Inside, the hush was as oppressive as fog, and Edward held his breath as he tiptoed upstairs. He was relieved to see that all the bedroom doors were closed.

Once he had pulled his own door shut behind him, Edward rolled back the rug and took a sheet of paper from his cache. Still angry with Duncan, he began to sketch a caricature of his brother marching with a musket on his shoulder. "I'll put a brick building with barred windows in the background," Edward whispered as he exaggerated his brother's chin and the stiffness of his spine.

When it was done, Edward printed *Dreaming of a Valorous Death* underneath it all. He was about to leave it on Duncan's pillow when he realized his anger was spent, and instead he opened the bureau drawer to put the drawing away. His eyes filled with tears when he saw his cousin's nightshirt. How many times in the past month had he slipped a drawing underneath it and never even thought of Wesley?

CHRISTMASTIME, 1864

Edward's eyes widened in surprise when he came into the dining room and saw Aunt Charlotte at her usual place at the table. This was the first time she'd left her room since the news of Wesley's death arrived more than a week ago. She seemed smaller, somehow, and her face was pale and drawn.

"Come sit down, Edward," she said. "Now that everyone's here we need to talk about tomorrow. It's Christmas, you know," she added when everyone looked at her expectantly.

Mary Beth broke the shocked silence that followed, asking with a catch in her voice, "How can we possibly celebrate Christmas so soon after—"

"It was his favorite holiday," Aunt Charlotte interrupted. "He wouldn't want you young people to miss what little celebration is possible because of—because of him." Her voice was steady, but her hand shook as she lifted her teacup.

Across the table, Becky's eyes were bright, and Edward was glad for her even though he knew it couldn't be much of a Christmas. He wished he hadn't dropped his plan to make everyone a drawing, because now he had nothing to give.

As though she could read his mind, Aunt Charlotte suggested, "Why don't you young people plan a little program as your gift to the rest of us?"

"Something appropriate for a wartime Christmas and a family in mourning," Mother quickly added.

She must be thinking of those riotously funny shows that he and Simon used to make up, Edward thought, and a familiar sadness stole over him.

"Let's make our plans right after breakfast," Mary Beth said, sounding almost like her old self. "We'll need every minute to rehearse."

But Duncan said, "You know I don't have time for that

sort of thing. You'll have to give me a part I won't need to practice."

No one spoke when he left the table, but after he had gone to get his coat, Becky asked brightly, "Aren't you glad Duncan has that job at the prison?"

A few minutes later, the three young people met in the chill of Uncle Gilbert's library, where they knew no one would disturb them. "What can we have Duncan do?" Mary Beth asked.

"Maybe he could read the Christmas story from the Bible," Edward suggested.

"And every few verses Becky can sing a carol—one that goes with what he's just read," Mary Beth agreed enthusiastically.

Edward searched his uncle's shelves until he found the book he wanted. "What about reading part of *A Christmas Carol?* You and I could take turns."

"Why don't you tell the story in your own words, and we'll pantomime the best parts?" Mary Beth suggested, her eyes shining. "You could be Tiny Tim, couldn't you, Becky?"

Becky nodded. "And Duncan can be Scrooge."

The three of them collapsed in laughter and couldn't stop even when Jocasta opened the door and glared at them.

"What do you want, Jocasta?" Mary Beth managed to ask.

"I wants to know if you done fergit dis is a house of mournin'!" she hissed.

Behind her, Aunt Charlotte said, "It's all right, Jocasta. Wesley wouldn't want them to mourn for him at Christmastime."

As the three chastened young people watched, Jocasta's

face crumpled. Aunt Charlotte put her arm around the weeping woman and gently drew her away, pulling the door shut behind them.

Mary Beth's eyes filled with tears, and Edward said brusquely, "You heard what your mother said. Now let's decide on the carols and figure out which parts of the story we can pantomime."

Wiping her eyes, Mary Beth said, "I'll copy the Bible verses for Duncan and leave a space where he should stop for Becky to sing. But I think it would be all right for you to make pencil marks in the book when you find the parts you want to tell."

Edward nodded. A few faint pencil marks would be nothing compared to what he'd done to other books in his uncle's library.

When he came into the parlor on Christmas afternoon, Edward was surprised to see how festive it looked. Duncan had cut some pine boughs and stuck them in a bucket of dirt, and Becky and Mary Beth had trimmed them with all the glass ornaments that would fit. There were no candles on the "tree," of course, but in honor of the holiday a fire burned brightly in the parlor fireplace.

Father had been given leave, and with him and Uncle Gilbert and Daniel all there, the room would have been filled with cheer even without the decorated evergreen boughs, Edward thought. The multicolored wool mittens and cap beside his plate at breakfast had been a nice surprise, but the best present he could imagine was having his father home for a whole day. Glancing around the parlor,

Edward's eyes came to rest on Father. He was thin, but he hadn't lost his look of youthful vigor. And beside him, Mother's happy face belied her black mourning clothes.

When Father raised an eyebrow inquiringly, Edward cleared his throat and said, "We have a program planned for you, and we want to dedicate it to Wesley's memory. First of all, Bible readings by Duncan and carols by Becky."

Duncan began to read, and Edward knew that in spite of what his brother had said the day before, he must have practiced. His voice was so mellow and expressive he sounded like a minister! Then Duncan paused, and Becky's clear, sweet voice began "Away in a Manger."

Later, as Becky sang her last carol, Edward noticed Jocasta listening in the doorway and hoped she had heard him say the program was in Wesley's memory. But there was no time to think of Jocasta—or Wesley—now. Becky and Duncan were leaving the room to join Mary Beth in the hall, where she'd laid out the costumes and props for the pantomime.

"And now we will present a narrated pantomime of *A Christmas Carol,* by Charles Dickens," Edward announced when Mary Beth signaled that all was ready. He took a deep breath and began to tell the story.

When it was over, Edward could hardly believe how well the program had gone. He hadn't forgotten anything, and Mary Beth had seen to it that each character came in at the proper time—and that two pot lids were struck together twelve times whenever she appeared as a ghost. Duncan had hunched over and worn an old top hat as Scrooge and stood tall in his uncle's coat as Bob Cratchit. And last of all,

Becky, her hair tucked inside a cap, had appeared without the stick she used for a crutch to say, "Merry Christmas, and God bless us, every one!"

After a chorus of voices from the audience echoed her words, Edward found himself the center of attention, with everyone congratulating him on how well he'd told the story. But all that mattered was Aunt Charlotte pressing his hand and saying, "Thank you, Edward. Wesley would have liked that."

Later, when the women were busy setting the table for a Christmas dinner Edward knew would be little more than corned beef boiled with dried peas, Father and Duncan pored over a map and talked about the Confederate defeat in the Battle of Nashville and the ravaging of Georgia by General Sherman's army. Edward tried not to listen, but he still heard snatches of conversation: ". . . Yankees in pursuit . . . little hope for us in the west now . . . Confederates abandoning Savannah . . ."

Edward's spirits sank lower and lower. Couldn't they forget about the war—or at least not talk about it—for just one day? He didn't blame Daniel for excusing himself on the pretext of looking for a book in Uncle Gilbert's library. Edward stared at the pattern in the parlor rug and wondered how Duncan could take such pleasure in talking about the war right after he'd read so convincingly about peace and goodwill.

Peace. The word seemed almost foreign to Edward. He could hardly remember when Virginia had been at peace, could hardly imagine that peace would come again. "Did you say something, sir?" he asked, suddenly aware of his uncle's voice.

"I asked how your artwork is coming along. It's been quite a while since I've seen any of your drawings."

Quickly getting to his feet, Edward said, "I can bring some down to show you."

"No need to bother. I'll come upstairs with you."

Becky, who had been leaning on the arm of Father's chair, jumped up and said, "I'll come, too."

Upstairs, Edward reached into the drawer for his stack of pictures, wondering uncomfortably how his uncle must feel, sitting in the room that had been Wesley's. Sitting in Wesley's chair.

With Becky hanging over his shoulder and giving a running commentary on the pictures, Uncle Gilbert looked at them all, studying some longer than others. When he had finished, he spoke for the first time. "I'm impressed with how much your work has improved, Edward. Is it because you have more time to draw now?"

"I think it's because of the paper shortage. That's forced me to work a long time on each drawing instead of starting over on a fresh sheet." Edward felt a sudden chill, remembering where he'd found the paper for some of the pictures he'd shown his uncle.

"If you ever run out of paper, Edward, you're welcome to use the blank pages at the backs of the books in my library. It would please me to think I'd played a small part in helping you develop your talent."

His uncle knew—and he wasn't angry with him! Relief swept over Edward, and then he was almost overwhelmed with regret that he had cut out the pages without asking permission. "Thank you, sir," he mumbled, too embarrassed to meet his uncle's eyes.

"You're very welcome," Uncle Gilbert replied.

"Did you know your face is red, Edward?" Becky asked. "Lean down so I can feel your forehead and see if you're feverish."

"I'm fine," Edward said, fending her off, "but let's go back downstairs where it's warm." Maybe by now Father and Duncan were through talking about the war. Maybe Father would ask what they had been doing and when he found out, he'd ask if he could see the drawings, too. Maybe, but probably not.

MID-JANUARY, 1865

Edward had begun to follow Jocasta again. It hadn't seemed a decent thing to do during the first weeks of grieving for Wesley, but life seemed almost normal now—as normal as it could be, anyway, with the city under siege. So Edward trailed along behind Jocasta every time she left the house, more convinced than ever that the woman was a spy. Not that she'd done anything suspicious. She was too smart for that. For two weeks now, she had always been on some errand for Aunt Charlotte. Until today.

Watching the brisk, purposeful way Jocasta moved, Edward sensed that today was different, and he wondered if this time the woman would look back to make sure she wasn't being followed.

Jocasta made an abrupt turn at a cross street and Edward ran to catch up, arriving barely in time to see her slip into an alley. He raced ahead to peer around the corner of the building and hardly had time to catch his breath before Jocasta turned onto the next street.

Edward sprinted through the alley, slowing again when he came out on the other side. There she was, walking along a dirt road not much wider than a path, when suddenly she disappeared into one of the small, weathered frame houses that lined it.

Glancing uneasily up and down the deserted road, Edward hoped Jocasta wouldn't be long. He scrunched down into his coat and decided to wait till he saw her come out with her bundle of food and then dash home ahead of her. He leaned against the wall of the building and hugged his arms across his chest.

When he was moving, Edward hadn't felt cold at all, but now his feet were almost numb. What if he couldn't run when Jocasta came out? He stamped his feet and considered leaving, but then he thought of the men in the trenches. If they could brave cold like this day after day, surely he could stand it a little longer.

Finally, though, he gave up and headed back through the alley. As he retraced his steps, Edward wondered if he should tell Aunt Charlotte about Jocasta's suspicious behavior right away or wait to see how the woman would explain her long absence. By the time he reached home, he'd decided to wait. He was about to slip quietly into the house when to his surprise Jocasta opened the door and said, "'Bout time you come home! Miss Becky, she keep askin' where you be, an' I keep sayin' I don' know."

But she did know, Edward thought, his heart sinking. She must have gone out the back door of that house, laughing to herself about the fine trick she'd played. Anger welled up in him, but it was quickly replaced by despair. Now that Jocasta knew he was following her, how could he ever prove she was a spy?

The doorbell rang three short rings, and Jocasta went to open the front door for Daniel. Edward heard her say, "Come on in, Marse Daniel, an' hurry on downstair to de fire."

"That fire's going to feel mighty good," Daniel said. "I think it's getting colder by the minute."

"Too cold to be standin' in de alley," Jocasta muttered as she brushed past Edward.

She'd be sorry, he thought, seething with anger as he followed Jocasta and Daniel downstairs to the warm kitchen. He wouldn't rest until he had his proof.

Jocasta was raking potatoes out of the coals when Mother and Aunt Charlotte came home from volunteering at the hospital. They both looked exhausted, but Aunt Charlotte managed a warm smile for Daniel. "How are you boys on the line getting along?" she asked.

"Just waiting for spring, Miss Charlotte. We're used to being hungry, but I don't think we'll ever get used to the cold and the damp."

"Will you be able to hold out till spring?" Mother asked, her voice worried.

Daniel shrugged. "Don't have much choice. It's hold out here or be shipped off to some Yankee prison."

"Yankee prison?" Edward echoed.

Nodding, Daniel said, "Every night, more men cross over to the Yankee lines because they can't face the cold and the hunger any longer. And the shelling and sniping."

"You mean they *desert?*" Mother asked incredulously. "That's disgraceful!"

"I don't think it's a disgrace, Miss Emily. There's only so much a man can take."

"Are you going to desert, Daniel?" Becky asked, her eyes wide.

He shook his head. "I prefer the evil I know to the evil I don't know," he said.

"This whole war is evil!" Aunt Charlotte burst out. "Subjecting our men and boys to unspeakable misery and—and death."

Edward was glad when Jocasta said quietly, "Supper on de table, Miss Charlotte. I'se savin' back a tater for when Marse Duncan come home from de prison."

Quietly, they gathered around the table, and Edward tried not to show his surprise and disappointment that the baked potatoes and "coffee" ground from charred corn kernels were the entire meal again tonight. Clever Jocasta must be holding back the food she'd gotten as payment for her information, trying to make him think he was mistaken about her spying.

Edward was still hungry when he'd finished supper, and he wondered if by now Mother was glad they hadn't bartered potatoes for his tuition at the academy. It was lucky she was too proud to send him to one of the free schools, he thought, because if he were in school all day, he wouldn't be able to follow Jocasta.

Later, when the servant woman left the basement kitchen, Edward said tentatively, "Aunt Charlotte, Jocasta was gone most of the afternoon while you were working at the hospital."

"I know. Her mother isn't well, and she went to visit her."

That explained today's trip and the meager supper, Edward thought, glad he hadn't told Aunt Charlotte his suspicions. Well, after what Jocasta had heard from Daniel at suppertime, she was bound to tell her Yankee contact how poor morale was on the Confederate line. He'd have to watch her every move.

Beginning right now! Edward had assumed when Jocasta went upstairs that she was going to bring in fuel for the fire, but now he saw that the coal scuttle was almost full. He left the half-finished drawing of Daniel on his chair and headed for the steps, trying to be quiet without seeming furtive. Once he reached the hall, he ran on tiptoe to the back door and opened it a crack. He was just in time to see Jocasta go out the gate. Dressed all in black, she was a darker shape against the darkness, a shape that moved off in the direction of the river.

Edward dashed for his coat, pulling it on as he hurried toward the door. His hand was on the knob when a voice behind him said, "And just where do you think you're going, young man?"

He wheeled around to face Aunt Charlotte, frustrated by the delay but half hoping his aunt would forbid him to go out into the cold darkness. "I—well, I—" He hesitated, wondering if he should tell his aunt about Jocasta's treachery. She'd practically asked, but—

"I'm waiting, Edward."

"I was going to follow Jocasta and prove that she's a spy. She—"

"Jocasta? *A spy?*"

Edward nodded. "She trades information to the Yankees for food—information she gets by listening when Uncle Gilbert or Daniel are here. How else do you think we eat as well as we do?"

"You listen to me, young man," Aunt Charlotte said, shaking her finger at him. "We eat this well because Jocasta goes out to meet one of the farmers who poles a flatboat down the Appomattox with food intended for our army. Food that ends up being sold to the highest bidder instead, making dishonest Confederate officials rich instead of feeding our soldiers, I might add." Aunt Charlotte's voice shook, and she paused a moment to compose herself. "Since Jocasta pays with U.S. coins," she went on, "this farmer's more than willing to trade with her. A spy, indeed!"

Edward felt limp. "I—I was sure she was a spy," he stammered.

Aunt Charlotte's voice softened. "You have a good imagination, Edward, just like my Wesley did. Now, put away your coat and come back to the fire, and we'll forget this ever happened."

As he followed his aunt down the stairs, Edward knew he'd never be able to forget his mistake. But at least no one else would know about it. How could he have faced Becky's endless questions or Duncan's scornful comments? And how could he have faced Jocasta if she knew *why* he'd been following her?

No one seemed to notice Edward slip into his chair.

Ignoring the lively conversation around him, he sat staring into the fire. He felt foolish, but worse than that, he felt useless. He'd been wrong about Jocasta, but she'd been right about him. *"I knowed de minute I done set eyes on you dat you was useless."* He remembered her very words, and he knew that they were true.

JANUARY 29-FEBRUARY 6, 1865

"Look!" cried Simon, pointing toward the Confederate line. "Over there, to the right!" His field glasses were trained on a white flag raised over the parapet of the Rebel works.

Bugle notes sounded in the distance, and beside him, Gabriel said, "It looks like they're sending over a messenger!"

A ripple of excitement ran along the Union line, and it wasn't long before word spread as though by telegraph: The Rebels had sent a letter for General Grant.

"Dear God, let it be about peace," Gabriel prayed, "so we can all go home to our families."

When peace came, Gabriel would go home to his family! "I never should of let myself start to care about him," Simon whispered as he watched Gabriel walk away. Turning toward the Rebel fort again, he stood staring across the shell-plowed open ground between the lines. . . .

Two days later, Simon stood atop the fort's crowded parapet. But unlike the soldiers watching the road for the first view of the peace commissioners who were coming from Richmond, he was looking toward the Rebel earthworks.

All of Petersburg must have turned out, Simon thought, adjusting his field glasses. Even though he knew it wasn't likely that Edward would be waiting on the Rebel parapet opposite where he stood, Simon had to look for him anyway, just in case. He scanned the rows of expectant faces until he heard cheering in the distance and felt a current of excitement sweep through the men around him.

Shifting his field glasses, Simon saw a carriage—no, a line of carriages—approaching. He kept his glasses trained on them as the one in front left the others and came through a break in the Rebel earthworks. Now, what had sounded at first like a dull roar from the Rebel side became clearer. It was a single word, repeated over and over again. Simon's heart leaped when as one, the men around him joined in with their own cries of "Peace! Peace! Peace!" and he shouted with them, "Peace! Peace!"

The carriage jolted across the scarred no-man's–land between the trenches, and a cheer went up. Now the air on the Rebel side was full of fluttering handkerchiefs, and on both sides hats were waved or thrown high. Simon snatched off his wool cap and shook it above his head and shouted even louder. Across the lines, Edward was cheering and shouting too—Simon was sure of it.

The shouts continued long after the carriage was out of sight, and when Simon stopped, hoarse, he could still hear cheers farther down the lines. Puzzled, he turned to Gabriel. "If we want peace, and the Rebels want peace, how come we're still fighting each other?"

"Because the men in the trenches aren't the ones who

decide. It's up to the leaders in Richmond and Washington."

Simon knew the men in the carriage came from Richmond, and he knew they'd come to meet with men from Washington and talk about peace. Suddenly he felt lighter. He was sure the fighting would be over soon. But then his heart sank. In the excitement of the moment he had forgotten that when the war ended Gabriel would go home to his family.

Beside him, Gabriel spoke again. "If this conference does lead to peace, what will you do? Have you any plans?"

Simon shook his head. He'd just trust his wits and do whatever seemed best for him at the moment.

"Good, because when the war ends, I want you to come back to Philadelphia with me," Gabriel said. "My wife and daughters will welcome you, and when you aren't in school, you can help in my print shop."

Simon's spirits soared. He wouldn't lose Gabriel after all! And he'd have things he'd never dreamed of—a home and family, a chance to go to school. He'd even be learning a trade! But all he could bring himself to say was, "Thanks, Gabe. I'll work hard for you."

Edward burst into the house and held up the newspaper so everyone could see the headline: PEACE CONFERENCE FAILS!

Duncan reached for the paper. "Let me have that," he said, his voice tense.

"Read it aloud," Mother urged, but Duncan ignored her.

At last, without looking up, he said bitterly, "Lincoln

refused to negotiate with our peace commissioners. He says there will be no peace talks until the South comes back into the Union."

"Maybe we should do it," Edward ventured. "Independence won't mean much if the Yankees have killed all our men and destroyed our cities." If they've killed Father and Uncle Gilbert, he added silently, and if they've destroyed Petersburg.

Duncan turned on him and said hotly, "You don't know what you're talking about! Where would we be today if the patriots at Valley Forge had given up against the British? Besides, if we give up now, it would make a mockery of the sacrifices the South has made over the last four years. It would all be for nothing."

The vehemence in his voice silenced Edward, but Aunt Charlotte said flatly, "You're wrong. It's the suffering and dying between now and the day our government in Richmond comes to its senses and meets Lincoln's demands that will be for nothing."

And Mary Beth added, "Daniel says more and more men are deserting every day and it's only a matter of time till General Lee has to surrender. I just don't understand why we keep on fighting if there's no way we can possibly win."

Duncan crumpled the newspaper and threw it down. "You certainly *don't* understand," he said. "We don't *have* to win. We only have to hold out until the North realizes they can't beat us. I agree with Jefferson Davis—death is better than surrender."

Edward watched his brother stalk out of the room. How could the Confederate president have said that? And how could Duncan believe it? Edward picked up the newspaper and began to read about the conference. He was so intent on trying to make sense of what had happened that he wasn't aware of anything around him until he heard Mother cry out. He looked up and saw Duncan standing in the doorway, wearing his coat and looking defiant, and he knew at once what his brother was about to do.

"I'm joining the men in the trenches," Duncan announced dramatically. "I'd never be able to live with myself if the South surrendered and I hadn't done my part."

Mother burst into tears, and in a few quick steps Duncan was at her side, patting her shoulder awkwardly. But when she clung to him, he pulled away. He bent to kiss Becky, gave Edward a scornful look, and left the room without so much as a glance at Mary Beth or Aunt Charlotte.

A moment later, the front door closed behind Duncan, and Mother wailed, "He's throwing his life away!"

"Get hold of yourself, Emily," Aunt Charlotte said sternly. "You're frightening Becky."

"Why Duncan?" Mother sobbed. "Why?"

Edward stared down at his sketch, wishing he were somewhere else. *Anywhere* else. He heard the controlled anger in his aunt's voice as she said, "Stop this shameful display at once and come upstairs, Emily."

When he heard the women leave the room, Edward raised his eyes to see Mary Beth trying to comfort Becky. The little girl raised a tearstained face and asked, "Is Duncan going to be killed like Wesley was?"

Edward felt as though a cold hand had closed around his heart. "I—I don't know, Becky."

Mary Beth said shakily, "There usually isn't much fighting in the wintertime."

Just freezing and starving, Edward added silently.

"How long is it till spring?" Becky asked.

"Weeks and weeks," Mary Beth said, wiping the little girl's face with her handkerchief. "Now go get the cards, 'cause we're going to teach you a new game."

Edward didn't particularly enjoy playing cards, but it was better than answering his sister's questions. Or thinking. He pulled his chair up to the table and waited numbly for Becky to bring the cards so he could shuffle them.

MID-FEBRUARY, 1865

Edward stood in line, waiting for the commissary to open. Snow had begun to fall, collecting in the bottom of the bucket he'd brought to carry home the beef the army allowed each household to buy once a week. He suspected it would be mostly soup bones again, since the troops and the Confederate hospitals—the hospital for the Yankee prisoners, too—were given priority when supplies reached the city.

Glancing up at the lowering sky, Edward hoped the snowfall wouldn't last long. Other years, he'd have welcomed a snowy day so he and Simon could build snow forts and have a snowball fight. But this year's forts and battles were real ones, and snow meant added suffering for the soldiers defending the city. For Father and Uncle Gilbert and Daniel. For Duncan, too, now.

Back at Riverview, Edward had never thought about soldiers suffering from the cold. He couldn't help but be aware of it now, though, with ill-clad soldiers in the streets and Mother making no effort at all to hide her fear for Duncan. It struck Edward that his mother and her sister were no more alike than he and Duncan were, and somehow that made him feel a little better.

Edward shivered as the line inched toward the commissary building. He felt a little self-conscious waiting among the servants and housewives, but Aunt Charlotte had asked him to do the errands this week because Jocasta's throat was raw and sore. Edward stamped his feet and hoped she would be better soon. This was the second time he'd stood in line for her—yesterday he'd collected the weekly ration of rice the Confederate government provided for each family now that food was so scarce. Holding his mittened hands to his face, he tried to warm them with his breath.

Women were coming out of the commissary now, and the line moved forward. When one of the returning servants passed him, an arm outstretched to balance the weight of her bucket, Edward glanced down to see what she was carrying. He recoiled when he saw a steer's bloody head, the horns resting on the bucket's rim.

Behind him a voice said, "Buck up, young man. It cooks into a fine soup. Makes as much sense to eat a cow's head as a pig's thigh, don't you think?" Turning around, Edward looked into a pair of bright blue eyes that peered from a wrinkled face. In response to his puzzled look the woman added, "You do eat ham, I daresay."

"Yes, ma'am, but I never thought of it as being a pig's

thigh." But however Edward thought of it, the image of a slice of ham fried until the fat along the edge was crisp and brown made the saliva start to flow.

It was hard to believe that only a year ago, having enough to eat was something he'd simply taken for granted. Having enough to eat and being warm. Edward thought of the meager coal ration available to each household, and he longed for the comfort of a huge, crackling fire and the homey sound of logs settling on the grate.

It was snowing harder by the time Edward had reached the door of the commissary building, and the flakes clung to the wool of his coat in a fuzzy layer. As he steeled himself to receive his steer's head, he thought about what the old woman had said. She was probably right, he decided, but he hoped his mother never found out what gave Jocasta's soup its meaty flavor.

In spite of the cold, Simon was damp with sweat by the time he came out of the sutler's hut clutching the magazine Gabriel had wanted and the dried fruit Henry and Julian had chipped in to buy. Until today, Simon had enjoyed running errands for the men, liked being trusted with their money. He hadn't even minded that the sutler always ignored him as long as possible before allowing him to pay, because he liked to listen to what the men were saying.

The white soldiers in the shop usually ignored Simon, too, but that didn't bother him at all. It was better than what had happened just now. He'd struggled to keep his face from showing the fear he felt when a private from a New York unit jostled and taunted him while he waited for the sutler to take his money. It had made him think of that terrible time when the men gathered around him, chanting "HIGH-er! HIGH-er!" while he tried to escape the heavy boots that stomped at his feet.

This time, there had only been one of them, Simon reminded himself, taking deep breaths of fresh air. Besides, it was over.

Suddenly a commotion some distance ahead caught Simon's attention, and he stopped to pull the field glasses from his coat pocket. His eyes widened when he saw that a group of soldiers, bored by the monotony of life in winter camp, had managed to scrape up enough snow to have a lively snowball battle.

As Simon watched he thought of the snowy day three years before when Duncan had declared that he and Edward were challenging their servants to a snowball fight. Simon smiled, remembering how in wordless agreement he and Ambrose had pelted only Duncan, and Edward had made sure all the snowballs he threw at the two of them fell short.

At the sound of excited voices, Simon lowered the glasses and looked over his shoulder. The sutler was standing outside his hut, grinning, while the rude private talked excitedly to one of the provost guards. When Simon saw the private point at him, the back of his neck prickled, and without thinking, he began to run.

"Halt!" The shouted command brought Simon to a stop. He knew what could happen when a person ignored that order. His package in one hand and the field glasses in the other, Simon waited, his heart sinking, while the guard strode toward him. "This soldier claims you're a thief," the officer said, nodding to the grinning private who had followed him.

"No, suh! I pay fer dis," Simon said.

But the officer's eyes were on the field glasses. "Hand over those glasses, boy, and be quick about it," he said.

"No! They're mine!" Simon cried, forgetting to use dialect as he clutched them to his chest. But the officer wrenched them from his hand, gave them to the soldier, and walked away.

"They ain't yours no more," the private said. He held up the field glasses for the sutler to see, then turned back to Simon and said contemptuously, "Now git out of my sight."

The wave of anger that swept over Simon gave way to a sense of helplessness, and he choked down a sob. It wasn't fair! Nearly blinded by tears, he headed for the Union line.

Back at the fort, Simon crawled into the bombproof and poured out what had happened. "If those men hate Negroes so much, why are they fighting to free the slaves?" he asked when he finished.

"They aren't," Gabriel said. "A lot of them wouldn't be fighting at all if they hadn't been drafted, and some of them are fighting to keep the South part of the United States. 'To save the Union,' as they say."

Simon frowned. He'd always thought "Union" was the name of the northern army, and he had no idea what "drafted" meant. "Well, I'm not goin' back to that sutler's ever again," he said.

Henry and Julian nodded silently, but Gabriel leaned forward and said, "You *must* go back. If you let your fear and anger and hurt keep you away, the sutler and that lying, thieving soldier will have won. But if you go back, they'll know that they can't scare you off." His voice grew more intense as he said, "They'll see that black people don't scare off. That we go about our business even when they make it hard for us." Gabriel paused, then added quietly, "There's more to freedom than not being a slave, you know. There's self-respect."

Simon stared into the small, smoky fire that did little more than take the chill off the air in the bombproof the men shared. He'd always thought freedom meant not having to do anything you didn't want to. That it meant doing whatever you liked, coming and going as you pleased. Slowly, he raised his eyes and saw that the others were watching him, waiting for his response.

"I'll go back," he muttered. He'd do it for Gabriel, and to show that black people would stand up for their rights. "I'll go back," he repeated, louder this time. He wasn't quite sure what self-respect was, but he was pretty sure that his decision had won the respect of his friends. . . .

The next day, Simon trudged through the camp, clutching the money the men had given him to buy some of the little cakes they liked so well. As he approached the sutler's, a tall corporal with a sandy mustache came out.

"Hey, you," the soldier called, reaching into his pocket. "I've got something for you."

Simon's eyes widened when the soldier pulled out a pair of field glasses and said, "Thought you'd want these back."

Simon's hand shook as he reached for them, and he knew if he tried to thank the man, his voice would shake, too. He raised his eyes to the corporal's face and saw an understanding smile.

"All the bigger fellows picked on me when I was a boy, and nobody ever stopped 'em," the corporal said. "I decided that once I was grown, I'd not stand by if I saw a youngster being bullied."

Simon managed to stammer his thanks, and he slipped the field glasses into his coat pocket as he watched the soldier walk away. Inside the sutler's hut, he had to wait even longer than usual before the man would take his money, but he didn't care. He had the field glasses back, and that was all that mattered.

MARCH, 1865

Edward sometimes wondered if the March rains would ever end. The dampness made the house seem even colder, and the family sat huddled in the kitchen, wrapped in quilts. The women were trying to fashion pieces cut from the upstairs carpet into soles for Mary Beth's worn shoes, and Edward was sketching Becky as she sat near the fire with her doll cradled in her arms. Poor Becky, he thought. So thin and listless.

A series of urgent rings sent Jocasta grumbling up the stairs to answer the front door. Moments later, Edward heard first men's voices and then Jocasta calling, "Miss Emily! Come quick—dey done brung Marse Duncan home!"

Mother gave a cry and ran up the steps, with Aunt Charlotte and Mary Beth at her heels. Edward followed them, questions tumbling through his mind. Who had brought Duncan? And why? Would they have brought him here if he was dead?

At the top of the stairs, Edward glanced back and saw Becky clutching her doll and looking up at him, her face filled with apprehension. "Wait there, Becky," he said. Then he squared his shoulders and opened the door into the hall.

It was Daniel and another young soldier who had brought Duncan, carrying him between them with his arms slung across their shoulders. As they lowered him into a sitting room chair, he slumped sideways.

"He took a chill, Miss Emily," Daniel explained, breathing hard after his exertion. "With all this rain, the trenches filled up and we've been waist-deep in water."

Mother didn't seem to hear Daniel. "Get him out of those wet clothes and then heat some broth for him," she instructed Jocasta. "Charlotte, you and Mary Beth fix a pallet by the fire." Her voice was firm, but her face was pale.

"We'll carry him down to the kitchen, Miss Emily," Daniel said, motioning to his friend.

Edward waited for the young men to come back upstairs, and after he had seen them to the door and thanked them for bringing Duncan home, he stood looking out the parlor window. In the foggy grayness, he could barely see the house across the street. Waist-deep in water in the trenches, Daniel had said. Poor Duncan. Would he have been so eager to "do his part" if he'd known what it would be like? Edward turned away from the window when he heard someone come into the room.

Mother moistened her lips and said, "He's delirious from the fever. If it goes much higher—" She drew a shaky breath and said, "I need you to go to the hospital on Washington Street, the one where your aunt and I volunteer. Find Dr. Anderson, and ask him for quinine. And hurry! It's Duncan's only hope."

Glad for something to do, Edward grabbed his coat and set off at a run, pulling his cap and mittens from his pockets. He didn't slow his pace until through the fog he saw the yellow flag that identified the former factory as a hospital.

The stories he'd heard about arms and legs being piled in corners while surgeons amputated shattered limbs nagged at Edward's mind as he stopped outside the building to catch his breath. That was in the field hospitals, he reminded himself as he opened the heavy door. In the field hospitals after a battle.

Inside, Edward's eyes traveled over the rows of beds until he saw a man bending over a patient. Tiptoeing down the narrow aisle between the beds, Edward kept his eyes straight ahead. "Dr. Anderson?" he said tentatively. The doctor turned to him and Edward said, "My mother sent me to ask for quinine for my brother." When the man shook his head, Edward cried, "But he'll die if you don't help us!"

Wearily, the doctor said, "I'd help you if I could, son, but right now all our hospitals are out of quinine and just about everything else. Maybe in a day or two—"

"But I need it right away!" Edward cried.

"Then you better ask the Yankees for it, sonny," called a soldier with a black patch over one eye.

The burst of laughter that followed this suggestion shook the last of Edward's composure, and he bolted from the building. Outside, the dampness clung to him, and he pulled his cap down over his ears and jammed his mittened hands into his pockets. But instead of starting home, he hung his head and let his despair flow over him. Mother would never forgive him if Duncan died.

The fog muffled the sound of a train whistle in the distance, and Edward scowled. It wasn't fair. While Confederate soldiers were hungry and their doctors were short of medicine, the Yankees' military railroad brought food right to their front line and carried their wounded back to a well-equipped hospital.

The Yankee hospital would have quinine! Without another thought, Edward sprinted toward the abandoned railroad track near the river. Slow down, he told himself when he reached it. He'd have to pace himself if he was going to follow the track the seven or eight miles to City Point.

But City Point no longer meant a sleepy village and Riverview, the peaceful plantation where he was born. Now City Point meant the headquarters and supply base of General Grant's Yankee army. Edward slowed to a stop. Maybe this wasn't such a good idea after all. He didn't know how to find the Yankee hospital, didn't know how he'd get the medicine once he was there. And what would he do if somebody stopped him?

Maybe he should just go home. Maybe— No. Mother was depending on him to get the medicine, and besides, he couldn't let his brother die because *he* was afraid. Edward squared his shoulders and started down the track, and to his surprise, he found that once his mind was made up, it was easier to control his fear.

The fog was thick near the river, and he welcomed its cover—it would help him slip through the enemy's line. He knew the railroad crossed the line next to the City Point Road, because he'd walked along the track with Michael when those earthworks were still part of the city's defenses. Before they were taken over by the Yankees who stormed across that open plain between the trenches and the woods in June.

Edward headed down the track, crossed through the thinly held Confederate line without being noticed, and walked on. Breathing hard now, he tried to estimate how far he'd come. It felt like he'd been walking forever, but in the fog it was hard to tell. He almost panicked when he heard the rumble of a train, but he quickly realized he must be approaching the point where the military railroad the Yankees had built joined the original track that had linked Petersburg and City Point. He was in enemy territory!

Edward could hardly resist the impulse to turn around and run back the way he had come. Think about the Yankees looking out the prison windows, he told himself. Think about the ones who were captured and marched through town the day of the explosion. They certainly hadn't looked dangerous.

But they hadn't had guns.

Edward's steps faltered, but he managed to continue on, reminding himself that he'd never heard of Yankees harming twelve-year-olds. He'd heard lots of stories about Yankee soldiers burning homes and even churches outside the city, stories about them forcing their way into homes and threatening the people inside to make them tell where their valuables were hidden. But nothing about—

Edward gave a start when the train whistled, signaling that it was coming to a stop. A daring idea came to him, and forgetting his fear, he began to run. He was out of breath by the time the hulk of the train materialized ahead of him. It was standing still, but Edward could hear the hiss of steam and knew the pressure was building up, ready to propel it forward again. His heart drummed against his ribs as he rested all his weight on the lever that opened the door of the last boxcar, then hauled himself inside.

In the dimness of the interior, Edward saw men wrapped in blankets huddled along the sides of the car, saw a bearded Yankee standing at one end with a rifle cradled in his arms. "Out," the man said, jerking his chin toward the open door. "This here ain't no passenger car."

The whistle blasted, signaling that the train was about to start, and Edward backed toward the opposite end of the car. "But sir," he said, hoping to stall until the train was under way, "you don't understand! I have to get to the hospital at City Point because my brother—"

"I understand you're gettin' off this train if I have to toss you off m'self," the man interrupted, starting toward him.

Edward struggled to keep his balance when the train jerked forward. If only he could stay out of the Yankee soldier's reach until the train was moving too fast for him to be "tossed off!"

Behind him, Edward heard a jarring crash, and when he looked back he saw the soldier sprawled flat. One of the men along the wall had tripped him! Edward stared, open-mouthed, conscious of the click of the iron wheels as the train gained momentum. Why would a Yankee want to help him? And then he noticed that beneath their blankets the men were wearing gray—Confederate gray.

The Yankee soldier hauled himself to his feet and grasped his rifle by the barrel. Sure that he would use its heavy wooden stock to strike the man who had tripped him, Edward cried, "Don't! I'll get off!" The words seemed to tear from his throat, and the Yankee paused to look at him in surprise. Only the clatter of the wheels, their cadence still increasing, broke the tense silence. Edward held his breath. *Why had he said that? How could he have put the welfare of a stranger ahead of his own brother's life?*

The Yankee soldier hesitated, rubbing his elbow, and then he pushed back his cap. "Don't see what harm it can do if one lad catches a ride," he said at last.

Weak with relief, Edward sank to the straw-covered floor and pulled his coat tighter around him. He was glad when the Yankee closed the boxcar's sliding door. The darkness would keep him from seeing the hollow faces and numb despair of the shrouded soldiers.

The Yankee struck a match and held it over his head, and then to Edward's surprise the man picked his way through the crowded car and squatted down in front of him. "When the train stops, you want to move to one of the cars in front of this one. That way you can ride the rest of the way to the hospital."

"Aren't you taking these men there?" Edward knew that Confederate prisoners were sometimes given medical treatment at City Point.

The man shook his head. "They're goin' to the wharf so we can load 'em on a boat for our prison at Point Lookout. We had a good run of Johnnies last night."

As the match flickered, Edward's eyes moved over the gaunt faces of the Confederates—a few of them defiant or ashamed, but most simply staring straight ahead. A good run of Johnnies? Slowly, the truth dawned on him. He turned to the Yankee soldier and whispered, "You mean these men are *deserters?"*

The match burned out, and in the darkness Edward heard no triumph in the Yankee's voice. "Aye, lad. Came across from their line—your line—last night. We fed 'em and warmed 'em up, and now we'll keep 'em till this cruel war's over. Can't be long, can it?"

A tide of conflicting emotions rolled over Edward. If the war was already lost, he couldn't blame these haggard men for being unwilling to freeze and starve for nothing. But it was because soldiers like these deserted that Duncan had joined the dwindling ranks in the trenches.

Waist-deep water in the trenches. Concern for his brother drove everything else from Edward's mind. He wasn't aware that the train was slowing until the Union soldier got to his feet, struck another match, and picked his way toward the lever that opened the door. As the train ground to a stop, Edward stood up, too, and his eyes met those of the grizzled soldier who had tripped the Yankee. Impulsively, Edward saluted. The man might be a deserter, but he was no coward.

Edward bent his knees, rested one hand on the floor in the doorway, and dropped to the ground. Through the fog he could make out the ghostly shapes of workers unhitching the boxcar, and he circled around them. Several cars ahead, he reached for the lever that opened the door, and his heart almost stood still when he hung all his weight on it and it didn't budge.

Edward pounded with his fist, but the sound could barely be heard, and, his panic rising, he searched the ground for something to bang with. He spied a half-buried rock and ran to pick it up. Frantically he tried to kick it loose, then pulled off his mittens and dug at it with his fingers.

The whistle blasted, and sobbing with frustration now, Edward ran alongside the train as it slowly began to roll down the track. The engine's smokestack belched flame and smoke, and gray ash blew back into his face.

"Hey, boy! Get away from there!" a voice shouted.

As the last boxcar began to rumble past him, Edward made a desperate lunge for the ladder that led to its roof, and he was dragged off his feet with such force he was sure his arms would be pulled out of their sockets. He could hear shouting as he lifted his dangling feet onto the bottom rung of the ladder.

Edward's throat was dry and his breath tore from his lungs in great gasps. The cold, damp air streaming past the train made his eyes water and swept the knitted cap from his head. Now he'd lost the cap as well as the mittens Mother had made him for Christmas.

His hands were so numb with cold Edward feared they would lose their grip on the ladder. With great concentration, he slowly, carefully relaxed his hold on one of the side rails and slipped his arm between it and the car, cradling the rail in the crook of his arm and wrapping his fingers around a rung. Then he repeated the maneuver with his other hand.

Edward gasped when the train rounded a curve. First he was afraid he'd be wrenched from the ladder and flung to the ground, but then he felt himself thrown forward and pressed against the boxcar. His jaws were clenched so tightly his whole face ached. It couldn't be much farther, could it?

Just when he thought he could stand it no longer, the whistle blasted and Edward sensed that the train was slowing. It braked with a rush of steam and a grating metallic screech, and as the train shuddered to a stop, Edward slumped forward, his body limp with relief.

But there was no time to waste—now that he was here, somehow he had to get the quinine. And then he had to get back home with it. Raising his head, Edward saw men with stretchers streaming past him to unload the sick and wounded, but to his dismay, he found that he couldn't relax his grip on the ladder's rung.

"Is dat you, Marse Edward?"

Astonished to hear a familiar voice call his name, Edward turned and looked into the wrinkled face of the slave who had been the cobbler at Riverview. "Uncle Jonas!" he cried. "Oh, Uncle Jonas, please help me!"

After the old man had pried Edward's fingers loose, he listened to the boy's story and then led him to a building at the back of the huge hospital complex. "You wait right here, Marse Edward, an' don' you worry 'bout a thing. I git dat quinine for you an' be right back."

Edward felt drained. He sank down onto the top step of the building to wait, glad to be able to turn his problem over to Uncle Jonas. To depend on him the way he'd depended on Simon in the old days. It was good to sit without thinking for a little while. Edward didn't want to think, because if he did, he would worry about Duncan—or about how he would get home with the quinine once he had it. The foggy grayness deepened, and Edward shivered.

At last Uncle Jonas returned and pressed the medicine into Edward's hand. "Now don' you worry none, 'cause dis gonna make Marse Duncan well," he said. "Jus' go down dis here road 'tween de buildin' till it end way down dere at dat road to de city. You be fine, Marse Edward. You be fine."

Edward choked out his thanks and turned away. As he walked between the rows and rows of hospital wards, he was tempted to pinch himself to make sure he wasn't caught in some horrible dream. If it weren't for the vial of quinine in his pocket, he'd have wondered if the terrifying train ride had actually happened. The swirls of fog made everything seem unreal, and though he knew he couldn't be far from Riverview, he had no sense of where he was. He felt terribly alone.

"All I have to do is follow this road back to Petersburg," Edward whispered when he finally reached the last of the wards and left the graveled hospital street for the road. He trudged on, his coat collar turned up and his hands in his pockets, remembering the day last spring that the carriage had rolled along this very road, headed toward his aunt's house. It seemed a lifetime ago. It almost seemed like someone else's life.

The road turned slightly, and suddenly the muted glow of campfires shone through the foggy darkness. Confused, Edward slowed down and tried to make sense of the situation. The fires were in a single row, so it must be a defensive line to protect the Yankees' headquarters, he decided.

His scalp tingled as every reluctant step took him closer to the enemy. He remembered how he and Michael had hiked out of the city, well past the Confederate defenses, during the weeks before General Grant's army came. No one had stopped them when they left town, but sentries had challenged them on their return.

Edward swallowed hard. He shouldn't have any trouble here, especially since the men were probably busy cooking their supper. He tried not to think of his own dull hunger—or of anything other than following the road through the break in the Union earthworks.

The fog muffled the sounds of the Yankees' voices, so Edward knew no one was likely to hear him. But knowing that didn't seem to help, and it was only when he began to feel light-headed that he realized he was holding his breath. Trying to breathe normally, he concentrated on looking straight ahead through the grayness and pretending he was the only person for miles around.

When he could no longer hear voices from the camp, Edward figured he was safe, and his body slumped with relief. One more danger lived through, he thought. But he had relaxed too soon—a shape loomed ahead of him, and he saw the pale light of a single fire.

"Halt! Who goes there!"

Edward's throat tightened so that he could hardly choke out, "J-just a b-b-boy, sir!" Scarcely breathing, he raised his hands above his head as the soldier came cautiously toward him, rifle ready.

"What are you doing behind Union lines?" the sentry asked, eyeing him suspiciously.

"I've been to the hospital at City Point. My brother was taken there."

"Let's see your pass."

Edward made a great show of searching through his pockets. "I must have lost it, sir," he lied, adding in a rush, "I'm not a spy, though—honest!"

The sentry laughed and waved him on. "Even if you were, I doubt it would make much difference in the long run."

Deliberately, Edward walked at a measured pace, not letting himself give in to the impulse to run. He forced himself to breathe deeply, and before long his fear had subsided to a state of watchful alertness. He'd gone another mile when he heard the thud of hoofbeats. His heart pounded almost as loudly as he bolted from the road and threw himself flat on the ground.

With his eyes tightly shut, Edward lay scarcely breathing until a cavalry patrol thundered by, and he waited until the sound had died completely away before he picked his way back to the road. Wary now, he kept to the edge, but no more cavalry details passed him. He found himself leaning forward a little as he walked, straining his eyes and ears, alert to any danger.

After perhaps an hour with no more challenges, Edward smelled smoke. And then he became aware of a strange sound. Could it really be—singing? Realizing that he must be near the encampment behind the Yankee trenches, Edward's icy fingers curled more tightly around the vial of medicine in his pocket. He thought of Mother waiting anxiously for him to return, and he forced himself to continue.

Soon the road entered the camp, and Edward tried to

move confidently as he walked between the rows of huts. He wished the fog hadn't begun to lift, hoped that if anyone saw him in the darkness, he'd be mistaken for a Yankee drummer boy.

The singing had stopped, but as Edward passed a large log building with candlelight shining from the windows, a band began to play. The music brought him to a halt, and he was sure that fear had affected his mind. How could he be hearing "Dixie" deep inside Yankee territory? But he understood at once when the men began to sing a parody of the southern song:

> "Way down South in the land of traitors,
> Rebel hearts, and Union haters,
> Look away, look away, look away
> To the traitor's land."

Edward didn't stay to hear more. Clenching his jaw, he strode forward, and soon he could no longer hear the words—only the lively tune, and then, silence. Cold, damp silence.

Finally, the road left the sprawling Yankee camp. Edward was trying to estimate how much farther he had to walk when a sharp challenge rang out. How could he have forgotten there would be pickets posted in advance of the Yankee encampment?

Edward repeated the story of how he had gone to City Point Hospital to visit his brother, but the young soldier who had spotted him rocked back on his heels and sneered at him. "You expect me to believe that? You'll tell me the truth, if you know what's good for you."

Edward stared at the Yankee, his mind suddenly blank. Had he come this far only to fail?

"What's going on over here?" An older man left the fire and walked toward them, a steaming cup in his hand.

Finding his voice, Edward turned to him and said, "I'm on my way to Petersburg. I went to City Point to visit my brother in the hospital without telling my mother, and now I'm trying to get back home. And worst of all, I've lost my pass."

The man said, "Come warm yourself at the fire and have a bit of supper while I decide what to do with you."

Edward followed him toward the fire, stumbling a little on feet numb with cold. He sank onto a log drawn up to the fire and gratefully accepted the tin plate of stew the picket ladled from the pot. Its savory smell made Edward's mouth water, and he bent forward to spoon it up. The first taste of the thick, meaty gravy swimming with chunks of beef and potatoes made him forget everything else, and when he had mopped the plate clean with a hunk of bread, he looked up to find the pickets watching him.

The older man leaned forward to dip more stew onto Edward's plate, ignoring his weak protests. Now that the worst of his hunger was satisfied, Edward glanced around as he ate. He looked curiously at the barrier that protected the pickets—crude cylindrical baskets that had been woven from the limbs of saplings, filled with dirt and stacked two high. He could hardly believe that he was surrounded by Yankees and felt no fear of them. It was true—they were just ordinary men, even if they were the enemy.

"Guess you ain't had a meal like that in a while," the

soldier who had challenged him observed smugly when Edward had cleaned his plate a second time.

Ignoring him, Edward turned to the older man and said, "Thanks for the supper and a chance to warm up. I'd better start on home now."

"Not so fast there, young man. How do you plan to get past your own lines?" The picket cupped his hands around his mouth and shouted, "He-e-e-y, Johnny Reb!"

An answering shout floated across the still air: "He-ey, yourself!"

Spacing his words so they would carry clearly, the man called back, "A—boy—from—the—city—wants—to—cross—your—line."

Edward waited tensely until the voice came again: "Send—him—over."

"Go on," the Union soldier said, waving aside Edward's thanks.

The open space between the two picket lines seemed endless to Edward as he crossed the uneven ground, stumbling over frozen ridges of dirt and breaking through the thin layer of ice that formed over the water-filled furrows where artillery shells had plowed the soil. His feet were thoroughly soaked by the time he reached the Confederate picket post. He looked around him and saw that it was like the one he'd just left, except for one detail: No blackened bucket of beef stew hung over the fire.

A tall soldier wrapped in a blanket confronted Edward. "I can't see why anybody with good sense would want to come into Petersburg." He peered closely at Edward and asked, "You got good sense, boy?"

Edward grinned. Cold and hunger would never make this man desert the South's cause. "I live in Petersburg," he said, adding the explanation that had by now become almost automatic. "I've been to City Point Hospital to visit my brother."

"Your brother's a lucky man," said a weary voice from the other side of the fire, "bein' able to leave this place with both his life and his honor." The speaker, shrouded in blankets, sat close to the meager fire, his feet wrapped in rags.

"Go home, boy," said the first soldier. "Go on home where you can warm up."

No one challenged Edward as the road passed through the Confederate earthworks, and he drew a long, shaky breath. He could hardly believe that he'd done it, that he was safe at last behind General Lee's line.

But as he came into the city, the ghostly ruins of buildings destroyed by Yankee shells and the eerie echo of his own footsteps on the cobblestones made Edward's heart pound again, and he longed for the comfort of a thick blanket of fog. It was only when he reached the residential streets beyond the range of enemy artillery that he began to relax.

At last Edward was home. Almost overcome with fatigue now that his ordeal was over, he dragged himself across the porch and through the front door. Jocasta came up from the kitchen, and her eyes widened when she saw him. "An' where you bin all dis long time? Ain't yo' mama got 'nuf to worry her wi—" The flow of words stopped, but Jocasta's mouth stayed open when Edward held the medicine out to her.

"I got the quinine," he said. With satisfaction, he watched her expression change from anger and disgust to surprise to something he couldn't identify before it settled back into its usual mask.

"I take it down to her, Marse Edward," she said, snatching the medicine from him.

He wasn't too late! Filled with relief, Edward closed his eyes and leaned against the wall. Slowly, he slumped to the floor. A moment later he felt someone shake him, and with a start he looked up into Mary Beth's anxious face. He had the feeling his cousin was asking him something, but he couldn't seem to focus on her words. Then Becky was beside him, beaming and chattering, and there seemed no need for him to say anything at all.

"Ev'rybody move out de way so's I can git dis chile to where it warm." Jocasta bustled down the hall, and before Edward could protest, she had slung his arm over her shoulder and was half carrying, half dragging him down the stairs to the kitchen.

"Thank God you're safe—and that you brought the medicine," Mother said, looking up. "It's his only hope." She began to sponge Duncan's flushed face.

In front of the fire, Aunt Charlotte unwound Edward's muffler and unbuttoned his coat while Jocasta took off one muddy shoe and Mary Beth struggled with the other. Sprawled in the rocking chair near the pallet where Duncan tossed and muttered, Edward gave himself over to them. When Jocasta peeled off his wet socks and began briskly rubbing his feet, he winced and wished his mother would look after him instead of fussing over Duncan. But it was only when Mary Beth brought him a cup of camomile tea that he roused himself enough to resist.

"You drink dat tea, Marse Edward, an' den I warm up yo' supper," Jocasta said, stepping back so Aunt Charlotte could slip a towel-wrapped heated brick under his feet.

"I already ate." Edward's statement was followed by a flurry of questions, and he bent his head over the teacup to postpone answering. He was so very tired! But he looked up and managed a grateful smile when Mother tucked a quilt around him.

"I was worried when you were gone so long," Mother said. "I couldn't imagine what was keeping you."

"Dr. Anderson didn't have the medicine. He told me none of our hospitals had any."

"Then where did you get it?" Mary Beth asked.

"From that big Yankee hospital on City Point. Uncle Jonas—he's one of the Negroes from Riverview—works there now, and he got it for me."

Aunt Charlotte recovered first. "You mean you walked all the way to City Point and back?"

"I rode part of the way there on the Yankees' train. I had to walk all the way back, though. That's why it took me so long. I had supper with some soldiers doing picket duty," he added, hoping to ward off any questions about his train ride.

His ruse worked. "Oh, Edward! Should you have done that, with rations for our men so scarce?"

"It was Yankee pickets, Mother, and they had food to spare."

"And then what happened?" Becky asked.

"I walked the rest of the way home." Edward marveled at how easy he'd made it all sound. Pulling the quilt tighter around his shoulders, he wondered if he'd ever feel warm again.

Later, bone-tired but unable to fall asleep, Edward lay in bed and relived the day. He could hardly believe he'd done it, done what he had to do even though he'd been afraid the whole time. Suddenly his eyes opened wide. Uncle Gilbert was right—when he'd needed courage, he had found it.

MIDDLE TO LATE MARCH, 1865

Simon's breath rasped in his throat and he felt a jagged pain in his side, but he kept on running. In the distance, he saw a yellow flag with an H in the center flying over a long, canvas-roofed frame building—the field hospital. Simon ran toward it, struggling for breath and tormented by nagging questions. Why hadn't Gabriel stayed in the bombproof when the fort was shelled that morning? Why had he risked his life trying to help Julian and Henry when it must have been obvious that they were dead?

If *he'd* been there instead of at the sutler's, he'd have pulled Gabriel to safety. He'd have— A sob tore from Simon's throat. He'd have cowered in the bombproof, like he always did when the fort was shelled, and he wouldn't even have thought about Gabriel. All he'd have thought of was the shell that hit the blacksmith shed and killed Hephestus, and the one that barely missed *him*.

Simon was close enough now to see the wounded men lying on the ground and leaning against the trees outside the hospital. His chest heaved as his eyes scanned the area, looking for Gabriel. No one had to tell him that a Negro soldier would be among the last to be treated.

There he was. Simon picked his way between the wounded men until he reached his friend, but then he didn't know what to do. Gabriel sat with his back against a tree, his eyes closed and his face ashen. His right arm hung bloody and useless. It looked like raw meat, Simon thought, staring in horrified fascination.

As though he sensed Simon's presence, Gabriel opened his eyes, and his parched lips formed the word "Water."

Simon ran toward an ambulance wagon parked near the building and bent down to draw water from the keg that hung beneath it. Carefully, he carried a dipperful back to Gabriel. "Here's your water," Simon said, kneeling down. Gabriel's eyes opened, and the boy saw that they were dull with pain.

"Need—help," Gabriel whispered when Simon turned the handle of the dipper to him. Awkwardly, Simon held the dipper to Gabriel's lips, but when he tilted it, most of the water spilled.

"You gotta put your arm behin' his shoulder," a voice said.

Simon looked up to see one of the ambulance attendants watching him. "Can you help my friend? Please?" he cried, scrambling to his feet.

"He have his turn on de table, soon 'nough," the man said. "Jus' two more white men afore him." When Simon's eyes strayed to the white soldiers who lay in the clearing, the attendant lowered his voice. "Dem feller so far gone dey jus' git morphine so's dey can die peaceful-like. Ain't nothin' to do for 'em. Your frien' be all right long as he don't git 'grene."

Gangrene. Simon wasn't sure what that was, but he knew wounded men died of it.

"Cuttin' it off dis soon after he was hit, he prob'ly be all right." The attendant took the dipper from Simon and headed toward the ambulance.

Cutting it off? Slowly it dawned on Simon that the doctors were going to amputate Gabriel's arm. A rush of saliva filled his mouth, and he ran behind the building and was sick. As he leaned against the wall and waited for the world to stop spinning around him, he heard Gabriel call his name—and then he heard a terrible cry from inside the hospital. For a moment, Simon stood as if paralyzed, but when another cry tore through the air, he stumbled away from the building and fled.

Simon ran faster than he'd ever run before, and by the time he reached the fort he had escaped the echoes of the wounded soldier's anguished cries. But all through the long, empty night in the bombproof, somewhere deep in his mind he could still hear Gabriel calling for him.

Simon leaned against the frame wall of a hospital ward at City Point and breathed in great gulps of fresh air. He hated this place. Hated it! But he couldn't leave Gabriel now that he'd found him again.

The day before, when Simon forced himself to go back

to the field hospital, one of the orderlies told him Gabriel had been moved to the main hospital at City Point. And then the orderly said, "If yo' name Simon, he been askin' fo' you. He 'fraid you kilt in dat shellin' yesterday." That was when Simon knew Gabriel didn't remember what had happened, didn't remember that he'd run away.

And so today he had walked to the hospital here on City Point, the place Jake had died, the place he'd sworn he'd never come back to. Simon shuddered, remembering how he'd stood in front of that same middle-aged woman in the headquarters building an hour ago and watched her run her finger down the list the same way she had before. Except this time she was saying, "Jackson . . . Jackson . . ." His heart had almost stopped when her finger did, but then she directed him here.

Simon had gone into the ward and tiptoed between the rows of beds until he stood at Gabriel's side. Gabriel was lying quietly, only the ashen tone of his skin and his clenched left hand showing his pain. Fighting the impulse to slip away, Simon had whispered, "Gabe?" Gabriel's eyes had opened, and when he saw Simon, his left hand unclenched and moved toward him.

Remembering that now, Simon whispered, "This time, I stayed with him. This time, I didn't run." But he'd wanted to. Instead, he had poured out half a glassful of water from the pitcher that stood on the small stand by the bed. Awkwardly, he'd slipped his arm behind Gabriel's shoulders and helped him sit up enough to drink it. And then a doctor had stopped at Gabriel's bedside and said cheerfully, "Time to see how that stump is healing, Corporal." *That* was when he ran.

"But only a little ways," Simon muttered. "I stopped right here, just outside the door." He glanced up when he heard the crunch of boots on the graveled street between the wards, and hardly believing his eyes, he cried, "Uncle Jonas!"

The old man peered at him for a moment and then his face broke into a smile. "Seem like half of Riverview here now," he said, putting his hands on Simon's shoulders and beaming down at him. "Come to de hospital kitchen wid me, an' Serena, she feed you jus' like she use to. She cook fer de colored hospital now."

By the time Simon had been fussed over by Serena and had eaten a bowl of her chowder and several chunks of thickly buttered corn bread, he began to feel a little better.

"Yessir," Uncle Jonas said, "wid you here now an' Marse Edward here de other day, it make me think of de ol' slavery days back at de plantation. I 'member how de two of you come 'round de cobbler shop all de time, beggin' me fer a tale, an'—"

"Marse Edward? *Here?*"

"'Deed he was," the old man said, and he launched into the story of how he had found Edward clinging to the ladder on the boxcar. "Las' I saw of him, he on de way back wi' dat quinine in his pocket."

Simon could hardly imagine Edward doing anything so daring. "You think Marse Edward get back all right?" he asked.

Jonas looked surprised. "He know de way, don' he?"

Finding his way would be the least of Edward's problems, Simon thought uneasily. He'd never been questioned here behind the Union lines, but then he was invisible to the soldiers unless they wanted somebody to work for them—or somebody to pick on. But it might be different for a white boy.

"You never say why you here," Uncle Jonas reminded him.

"Friend of mine, dey brung him here," he said, a little ashamed that hearing about Edward had made him forget Gabriel. "I'se goin' back to him now," he added as he got to his feet.

Simon made his way back to Gabriel's bedside, careful to keep his eyes on his friend's face so that he wouldn't have to look at the bandaged stump of his arm. He saw that Gabriel's skin was starting to regain its usual dusky color and that the lines etched by pain had smoothed a little.

"Doc, he give him somethin' for de pain," the man in the next bed told Simon. "He sleep now."

Satisfied, Simon sat down on the floor by Gabriel's bedside. He stretched his arms out in front of him and stared at them, trying to imagine what it would be like to have only one.

A week later Simon stood on the bluff at City Point, his field glasses trained on the feverish activity on the wharf below him. Horses tossed their heads as they were led down the gangplanks of steamboats. Contrabands unloaded crates from barges and muscled them into wagons lined up along the edge of the dock or tossed bales of hay for livestock onto the flatcars of a train that stretched along the tracks on the forage wharf. And along the river, as far as he could see, boats lay at anchor, waiting to be unloaded.

It was a long time before Simon lowered his field glasses and headed for the point of land where the Appomattox River flowed into the James. Guiltily, he thought of the recovering patients he was teaching to read and spell. He knew they'd be disappointed to miss their lessons, but he couldn't have stood being cooped up in a hospital ward on such a glorious day.

"Education will give black people another kind of freedom," Gabriel had told him. But Gabriel hadn't said that helping them get that education would take away his own freedom to come and go as he pleased.

As Simon walked past the army's vast array of repair shops, he heard a familiar ringing sound, and willing himself not to think of Hephestus's fiery death, he stopped to watch one of the blacksmiths at work. The man's dark face dripped with sweat from the heat of the forge as he plunged the glowing metal into his water barrel.

"Gotta make all dese wagon fit to roll," he said when he saw Simon watching.

"How come, uncle?" Simon asked.

"Dis army movin' out o' here. Gonna take dat Petersburg dis time, an' dey sayin' if Gen'l Lee tries to 'scape, dey gonna go right after him," the smith said, pumping his bellows.

Simon watched the coals in the forge glow red again. "Boy I use to know, he live in Petersburg," he said tentatively.

"Don' worry none 'bout him. Gen'l Grant, he not gonna bother nobody but dat Lee an' de few soldier ol' Lee got left."

When the smith reached for his hammer and it was obvious that the conversation was over, Simon walked away, but it wasn't long before he stopped again, this time to watch a company of soldiers on the drill field. The sense of energy in the men's movements and the glint of sunlight on their bayonets made his heart beat faster. "Gettin' ready to take Petersburg an' go after Lee's army," he whispered, and suddenly he wanted to go with them.

The blacksmiths would be part of the wagon train that followed the army when it left—maybe one of them could use an experienced helper! Filled with excitement, Simon was heading back to the huge shed when he thought of Gabriel, and his steps faltered. Gabriel wouldn't mind if he went, Simon told himself. He was staying with Gabriel of his own free will, so he could leave of his own free will.

Now Simon could hear the *clang-a-lang-lang* of the blacksmiths' hammers above the noise of the steam engine he was passing, but something seemed to hold him back. It would be different if Gabriel had asked him to stay at the hospital, Simon argued silently, reminding himself that Gabriel had never asked anything of him.

But he had. Gabriel called for him, and he ran away. Ten days ago, he'd left Gabriel leaning against that tree outside the field hospital, and he'd run away from there as fast as he could. "I came back, though," Simon whispered. "I came back an' found him, an' he didn't remember anything about it." *He* remembered, though, and he was ashamed. He couldn't abandon Gabriel again.

Reluctantly, Simon turned away from the row of repair shops and walked on toward the point, but the day had lost its magic. By the time he stood overlooking the turbulent brown water where the two rain-swollen rivers joined, his earlier excitement was gone. All he felt now was a certainty that even when the war was over, he wouldn't have the freedom he had always longed for. He'd never be free to do just what he pleased. Never.

Simon sighed. A year ago he'd stood in this very spot with Edward and they'd looked down at the roiling water together. Was he any better off now that he was free? "Yes," he whispered, and then above the roar of the rivers he shouted, "Yes!" Suddenly it was clear to him: Now he was free to decide for himself.

A sense of calm settled over Simon, and he felt older. Wiser. He had weighed staying with Gabriel against following after the army, and he'd made his own decision. Things had changed since his brother told him to stick with the Union army. Now he was going to stick with Gabriel.

Simon raised his face to savor the warmth of the sun on his skin for a moment before he started back to the hospital where Gabriel—and his pupils—would be waiting for him.

APRIL 1-3, 1865

Edward lay staring into the darkness, listening to the continuous roar of artillery fire. There was always some shelling at night, but it had never been like this before. He dragged his quilt to the window and pulled the curtain aside. Huddled there, he tried not to think as he watched arcs of fire streak across the sky. Tracing the path of each mortar shell, he waited for its splash of fire and the lingering puff of white smoke it would leave against the darkness when it exploded. He wished he could light a candle and sketch the fearsome spectacle, but candles were far too scarce for that.

Edward was startled when a small voice said, "I'm scared."

"I didn't hear you come in, Becky," he whispered as he tucked part of his quilt around his sister. "Pretend you're watching fireworks, and it won't be so scary."

The little girl snuggled down next to him and confided, "Mary Beth has her pillow over her head, but when I tried that, I couldn't breathe."

They both gasped when flames blazed upward in the distance and billows of gray smoke stained the clear darkness of the night sky. Edward wondered what had been hit.

"I just noticed something," Becky said. "You see the flash of fire when the cannon goes off—there's one—but you don't hear the boom until . . . now!"

"It takes time for the sound to travel. Remember how you see lightning before you hear the thunder?"

"And you can count to see how far away the lightning struck," Becky said excitedly. "How does that work?"

"I think it's a mile away for every five seconds you can count before you hear the sound."

At the next spitting flame, Becky began to count. She had reached fifteen when they heard the boom. "That means those guns are a long way off," Becky said, sounding relieved.

Edward didn't answer. Three miles didn't seem all that far away to him. A sudden flash from the side window made Edward flinch, and then the firing seemed to be coming from all directions at once: *BADOOM! BADOOM! BA-BA-BA*-DOOM!

"Becky," he asked, struggling to keep his voice calm, "when you were in your room, could you see light from the shells exploding?"

She nodded, and Edward knew the defenses of Petersburg were being shelled from all parts of the enemy's line. His heart sank until it felt like a hunk of rock deep in his chest as he thought of Daniel in the trenches, thought of his uncle in a fort west of the city, thought of his father and wondered where he was tonight and whether he was safe.

The door opened and Mother whispered, "Is Becky with you, Edward?"

"I was scared," Becky piped up, "so I came in here."

"Charlotte thinks we should all dress and go downstairs," Mother said, her voice steady.

Edward pulled on his clothes in the cold darkness and then watched from the window in the upstairs hall, keeping his mind occupied by making mental notes so he could draw the fiery display later. One by one, the others joined him. By the time they were all there, the darkness had lifted enough that the silhouettes of trees and buildings stood out, black against a deep, deep blue.

Was the roar of artillery louder now, Edward wondered, or did he just imagine that it was? He followed the others down to the kitchen, where Duncan sat in a rocking chair near the hearth with Mother's shawl around his shoulders, and Jocasta knelt to coax a flame from the embers.

"Listen," Duncan said, holding up his hand, and obediently they all paused and cocked their heads expectantly. "Hear that?" he asked when there was a sudden break in the continuous spitting of rifle fire. "It's going to start up again in just a— There goes another volley, but it won't last long."

"How can you sit here in the kitchen and know what's going to happen out there?" Mary Beth demanded.

The sound died down abruptly, as Duncan had predicted, and he said quietly, "It's a charge."

Edward stared blankly at his brother until the meaning of his words began to sink in: The Yankees were charging the thinly held Confederate line, the line at the very edge of the city. Were there troops enough to force them back, or was this the day Petersburg would fall?

An hour later, they were all sitting silently around the kitchen hearth when Father came down the stairs. Edward could hardly believe his eyes. Father was safe! Thinner, but safe.

After the flurry of hugs and greetings, and after Duncan's half-proud, half-embarrassed account of his weeks in the trenches and how he had fallen ill, Becky asked shyly, "How long can you stay, Papa?"

"I shouldn't be here at all, but—" Father paused, then without meeting anyone's eyes, he said, "Lee's evacuating the city tonight. I'm to ride ahead to help protect the wagon train."

"Evacuating!" Mother cried. "General Lee's leaving Petersburg undefended?"

"There's no way he can defend it any longer, Emily." Father sounded resigned. "Two small forts that guard the road into the city are all that stand between Grant's army and the inner line west of here. And that line's stretched too thin to be much of a defense."

Aunt Charlotte's voice was shrill. "Why doesn't Lee surrender and get it over with? What good will it do to evacuate the city? That's like cutting off a dog's tail an inch at a time!"

Father looked taken aback at her outburst, but he answered, "My guess is that we'll join forces with General Johnston's army in North Carolina. Whether Grant takes Petersburg and Richmond won't matter as long as we still have an army left to fight him with."

Edward stared at Father. How could he say it wouldn't matter if Grant took Petersburg?

"If the men at those two forts can hold out long enough, it might give General Lee time to fortify the inner defense line," Duncan said eagerly.

"I think that's what he's counting on," Father said, looking at Duncan with approval. "It would give the rest of the army time to withdraw across the river."

"Jocasta will pack you some bread and cheese to take along," Aunt Charlotte said, and Edward saw Father give her a tired smile.

As soon as Father left, Aunt Charlotte went upstairs, and watching her, Edward frowned. Something about the way she moved disturbed him. "I wonder what's wrong with Aunt Charlotte," he said uneasily.

"She's probably worried because Uncle Gilbert's at Fort Gregg," Duncan said. "That's one of the forts that has to hold off the Yankees until Lee can move men to the inner line," he explained when the others looked puzzled.

Mary Beth gave a smothered little cry and ran upstairs,

and after a moment of shocked silence Mother said, "I'll go and wait with Charlotte."

"The survival of Lee's army depends on the men at those forts," Duncan said, nervously cracking his knuckles. "I hope they can hold off the enemy long enough to make a difference."

Edward stared at his brother. Didn't Duncan care about the survival of the men who made up Lee's army? Didn't he care about Uncle Gilbert? Stumbling blindly toward the stairs, Edward almost tripped over Becky, who sat huddled on the bottom step.

He burst out the front door and almost collided with his uncle. "Uncle Gilbert!" he cried, his legs weak with relief. "We thought you were at Fort Gregg."

"I'm on my way back there now, so I can stay only a moment."

"Aunt Charlotte and Mary Beth are upstairs," Edward said, somehow managing to keep his voice steady. He held the door open for his uncle, then sank down onto the porch steps and tried not to think. He had no idea how long he'd been sitting there in the chill of the April morning before Uncle Gilbert came outside again.

"I'm glad you're still here, Edward," he said, pulling out his pocket watch. "I'd like you to keep this safe for me."

Wordlessly, Edward stretched out his hand. Uncle Gilbert's watch! The watch that should have gone to Wesley. Edward's eyes filled with tears as his fingers closed around it and he felt the warmth of his uncle's body lingering on the ornate gold case. He pressed the watch to his cheek.

It wasn't until he heard the gate latch that Edward realized his uncle had gone. Holding the watch tightly, he ran out onto the sidewalk and stood watching until the tall, thin figure disappeared around the corner. Edward was still staring after him when a group of ragged, nearly barefoot Confederate soldiers came down the street, headed toward the river. Why did Uncle Gilbert have to stay behind? *Why?*

One of the neighbors in the little group gathered at the corner cried out and pointed down the street, and Edward turned to see what everyone was staring at. He caught his breath at the sight of dark smoke churning above a bank of flame. A pall of smoke drifted toward them, and he knew at once what was afire.

An old man's voice broke the silence. "Petersburg is doomed," he quavered, "and there's the proof of it."

Silently, the neighbors turned toward their homes, heads bent, and Edward ran to tell Duncan the news. "The Yankees are burning our tobacco warehouses!" he shouted as he pounded down the stairs.

"You fool!" Duncan said harshly, gripping the arms of his chair. "*We're* burning the warehouses so the Yankees won't get all the tobacco their blockade kept us from shipping out." Duncan slumped back in the chair and turned his face to the wall. "It's all over now," he said, his voice breaking. "There's no hope left."

Outside the city, Simon sat on the parapet of an abandoned Union fort and trained his field glasses on the blue-coated men surging across the muddy plain. It looked like the whole army was headed toward the two Rebel forts that guarded the western entrance to the city. This time it was going to happen, he told himself. This time, the Union army was going to take Petersburg. He'd watched the first battle, and now he was about to see the last—and with Gabriel's blessing, too. "Go and be our eyes," Gabriel had said, "then come back and tell us everything you saw."

Focusing his glasses on the larger of the forts, Simon studied first the wide moat that surrounded it and then the log palisade that topped its thick earthen walls. Already, Union artillery hammered the fort as the solid mass of blue swarmed across the plain, but no shots had been fired by the defenders. How long could the Rebels hold out? Simon hoped they weren't going to surrender without a fight. After his long trip from City Point—some of it bouncing along on the seat of a newspaper boy's cart—he wanted to see some action, something worth telling Gabriel and the other patients in the ward.

Suddenly, Simon saw flashes of rifle fire and two puffs of white smoke from the Rebel cannon. When the Union attackers fell back in confusion, leaving the ground covered with their dead and wounded, Simon began to wish the defenders *had* surrendered. The Rebel artillery thundered at measured intervals now, and each shell mowed down a swath of men. Simon heard cheering from the Rebel lines, and he saw that action had stopped all along the front while men on both sides watched the battle.

The Union troops retreated out of rifle range, and Simon felt the ground shake as artillery shelled the Rebel fort again. At last, reinforced, the blue-clad troops moved forward, and Simon strained his eyes, trying to see through the smoke. By the time it began to lift, Union troops had reached the moat surrounding the fort. Simon watched them plunge into it, holding their muskets high above the chest-deep water.

He cheered when a soldier thrust the staff of his regimental flag into the slope of the Rebel earthworks, but his cheer ended in a gasp when the man staggered backward into the moat. Simon watched him sink beneath the water, leaving a swirl of red on the surface.

Quickly shifting his field glasses, Simon focused them on the soldiers struggling up the steep sides of the earthworks. "Must be mighty slippery," he muttered as he watched them dig swords or bayonets into the muddy slope to keep from sliding down again. "An' how are they gonna get over that palisade at the top?"

A flurry of activity off to one side attracted Simon's attention, and his heart beat faster when he saw that the attackers had discovered an unfinished trench—a way into the Rebel fort! He watched the first Union soldiers reach the parapet, but his cheer stuck in his throat when they faltered and then pitched back onto the men behind them.

In fascinated horror, Simon watched one man after another reach the top, only to be forced back, stumbling over the bodies of the dead and wounded. But then Union soldiers were on the parapet, some firing into the fort, some hauling other men over the wall. "They must be fightin' hand to hand in there," Simon muttered. His head began to swim, and he was glad he couldn't see what was happening.

Sliding down from his perch on the parapet of the abandoned fort, Simon sank onto the firing step and leaned back against the earthen wall. He squeezed his eyes shut and listened to the din of battle. Somewhere in the city, he thought, Edward was hearing this, too. Hearing it and wondering what was happening. "He's lucky he doesn't know," Simon whispered.

At last the firing stopped, and he opened his eyes. Pulling himself to his feet, Simon climbed back onto the parapet and raised his field glasses again. When he saw the United States flag flying over the fort, his heart beat faster, but he couldn't bring himself to cheer. Not after what he'd seen.

He aimed the glasses beyond the captured fort toward the smaller one, realizing now that the battle had been raging there, too. While he watched, Rebels fled over the rear wall as Union soldiers swarmed in from the front. Tense with excitement, Simon watched the small band of gray-clad men run toward a defensive line just outside the city. But when he looked back expectantly, he saw that the Union troops had stopped some distance before the Rebel line.

"Go *on!*" Simon cried. What were they waiting for? They were so close! Disbelief—and then disappointment—flowed over him when he saw that the men were making camp. Abruptly, he turned away. He didn't want to think of all the weary miles he had to walk before he was back at the hospital. And then he'd have to tell Gabriel and the others that the army *still* hadn't taken Petersburg.

When Edward heard the sound of horses' hooves and metal wheels on the cobblestone street that night, he raised his head to look across the room at his brother. Duncan had insisted on coming upstairs to watch the army leave the city, and Jocasta had lit a fire in the parlor fireplace for the first time since Christmas.

"It's begun," Duncan said from the window, where he sat wrapped in a quilt. "The evacuation's begun."

Edward joined him and peered into the darkness. "The artillery's pulling out," he said when he saw the silhouette of a cannon.

Becky asked, "Do you think they'll all be able to escape before the Yankees find out they've gone?"

"They're not escaping, Becky," Duncan said sharply, "they're withdrawing. If Father's right, they'll join forces with General Johnston to fight Sherman's army and pay them back for what they did in Georgia."

Don't start in again on Sherman's march to the sea, Edward pleaded silently. Aloud, he said, "Becky, it's time for you to go upstairs to bed, and remember, you're to sleep in Mother's room tonight."

"That's so Mary Beth can cry for her papa," Becky said. "Will Mama come to bed soon?"

"She'll come after you're asleep," Edward said, managing to keep his voice steady. "Aunt Charlotte needs her now." Turning back to the window, he rested his forehead against the coolness of the glass, closed his eyes, and tried to block out the sound of Duncan's voice going on and on about the heroism of the men at Fort Gregg.

Slowly, Edward became aware that both the rumble of wheels and his brother's monologue had stopped, and when he opened his eyes, the dark shapes he saw outside were men hurrying past. Escaping, he thought dully. Becky had the right word for it.

In spite of the sound of men's voices, the occasional shouted order, and now and then the ring of hooves on the cobblestones, Edward's head soon began to nod.

"Look, why don't you go on up to bed? Put a little more coal on the fire, and I'll be fine," Duncan said.

Edward was glad to be alone in his room. Fully clothed, he lay on the bed, listening to the noise in the street and the growl of Union artillery in the distance until finally he fell asleep. He woke in the half-light to cries of triumph. Wide awake at once, he ran to the window and looked down into a street teeming with blue-clad soldiers. But to his surprise he felt no fear, only acceptance and sorrow.

Hearing whispers outside his door, he went into the hall to join Mary Beth and Becky and the women. "Look," Mary Beth said, pointing to the courthouse tower. "They've raised their flag."

Edward wasn't prepared for the rush of emotion he felt when he looked across the rooftops and saw the United States flag flying proudly in the distance. "It looks like it belongs there," he said at last.

"It does belong there," Aunt Charlotte said, her voice shaking, "and if that flag had never been torn down—"

"There now, Charlotte," Mother said, putting her arm around her sister. "It's over."

Over for us, at least, Edward thought. He hadn't forgotten that Father and Daniel were headed toward North Carolina with what was left of General Lee's ragged, hungry army. But for the first time in almost ten months, morning had come to Petersburg without the sound of shelling.

That afternoon, Edward stood looking out the front window of his room. The street below was deserted except for blue-coated soldiers at the corner and the occasional Negro. He glanced down at the boy walking jauntily along the sidewalk, a boy about Simon's size. For a moment, Edward's heart beat faster, but a closer look told him it wasn't Simon.

If only it *had* been Simon. If only— Wishful thinking never changed anything, Edward reminded himself sternly. Simon wasn't going to come looking for him. He'd made his choice almost a year ago, when he saw the Negro soldiers in the lane. "It doesn't matter," Edward whispered. "I don't need him anymore." He was surprised at the hurt he still felt. Not hurt, exactly, he decided, but something more like regret.

It didn't make sense, Edward thought. Jocasta worked harder for Aunt Charlotte than any house servant ever worked at Riverview, and yet she stayed. But Simon left even though he'd hardly had any work to do. And they'd always had such fun together! "I guess he didn't leave *me* so much as he left *slavery,*" Edward mused aloud. Simon had chosen freedom over slavery even though it had meant choosing freedom over friendship, too.

Edward frowned. Could it be that choosing was what really mattered? Was that why Jocasta had been so angry on the long-ago day when he'd mistaken her for a slave? Of course! That was why she'd made it so clear that she could leave Aunt Charlotte's anytime it didn't suit her—and why Simon had left even though life at Riverside surely must have suited him. Edward felt as though a burden had been lifted from him, a burden he'd carried for so long it had become a part of him.

A spring breeze blew the curtain, and his attention turned to the pale green of the budding trees. It was too nice a day to stay indoors, but with the city full of Yankee soldiers, no one was going out. A knock at his door interrupted Edward's thoughts. Becky. He waited for her to leave, but to his dismay, the knob turned and the door opened.

"Oh, I'm sorry!" Becky's hands flew to her face when she saw Edward. "I was looking for a place to be alone."

"We can be alone together, Becky," Edward said. He didn't blame the little girl for wanting to be away from the grieving women and from Duncan's gloom.

"What's 'a hero's death'?" Becky asked. "Duncan says Uncle Gilbert died a hero's death, but I don't know what that means."

It didn't mean anything, Edward thought bleakly, and then he remembered his uncle walking resolutely toward Fort Gregg the day before. Taking a deep breath, he said, "It means that he—faced death—bravely. He did his duty even though he knew it meant he'd probably be—" Edward broke off and turned away, forcing down the sob he felt rising in his throat.

"I think you should draw a picture of Uncle Gilbert," Becky said quietly.

Struggling to regain his composure, Edward went to the bureau and reached into the bottom drawer. "I did this one yesterday," he said, his voice steady as he handed his sister a picture that showed Uncle Gilbert holding his pocket watch by its chain and himself with his hands outstretched to receive it. His own face was hidden, and his uncle's was just the way he remembered it—regretful, but unafraid.

"He gave you his watch? Can I see it?"

Edward reached under his stack of drawings and lifted it out, noticing how cool the gold case felt now.

After she admired it, Becky asked, "Can I look at the rest of your pictures?" Her eyes were on the one that showed the furious shelling of the city two nights before.

"Yes, but only if you promise not to say another word." Edward picked up his stack of drawings and searched through it till he found the one he wanted, then handed the rest to Becky. He waited until the little girl had settled herself in a patch of sunlight on the floor before he sat down and began to study the drawing he'd picked out, the one he'd done of Jocasta months ago.

That was how he'd seen her then, he thought, but now—He paused, eraser in hand, reluctant to change the best work he'd ever done. He'd draw another picture instead, he decided, rolling back the rug to take a sheet of paper from his cache. He waited, his eyes closed, until he had a clear image of Jocasta in his mind, then opened his eyes and bent over the paper.

Edward sketched quickly, and when he paused, he saw that the woman's stance was proud now, not challenging. He would make her face sad, tragic even, but not defiant. Yes! It was coming. Breathing shallowly, he drew her wearing a shawl, one hand at her throat, and in a flash of inspiration he drew a basket for her to cradle in her other arm. "To show how well she provided for us," he whispered as he filled the basket with vegetables and loaves of bread. His face grew warm at the memory of how he had suspected Jocasta of spying for the Yankees. He added a few finishing touches and sat back to look at the finished drawing.

"Can I see?"

Startled, he nodded. He'd been so engrossed that he'd forgotten Becky was there.

"Why, that's Jocasta!" the child exclaimed. She picked up Edward's earlier drawing and studied it. "You did this one when she was being so mean to you," she said at last. "I wonder when she changed?"

Edward knew the answer to that: It was when he brought home Duncan's medicine and Jocasta decided he wasn't "useless" after all. That had changed the way she looked at him, and the way he looked at himself, too. But it wasn't the sort of thing you talked about with your little sister.

"What are you going to do with that one?" Becky asked when she saw that Edward had kept out the new drawing of Jocasta after he put the others away.

"I'm going to give it to her," Edward said. Silently, he added, She'll know it's a peace offering.

EARLY MAY, 1865

The packet boat steamed away, leaving the little group standing silently on the wharf below Riverview. Bewildered, Edward looked from the maze of piers and loading docks to the hulking warehouses. No wonder the Yankees had won! Compared to all this, the Confederate headquarters and their quartermaster's stores were nothing.

Edward raised his eyes expectantly to the house on the

bluff, but it stood stark and unwelcoming. One of the shutters was missing, another hung from a single hinge.

"Well, are we going to stand here all day?" Duncan asked.

Becky took her mother's hand and led her toward the shore. Edward and Duncan followed them, leaving behind the trunks and a barrel of provisions from the Union commissary. Their steps echoed as they walked along the wooden wharf.

Nothing looked familiar. It was as though he had never been here before, Edward thought as he crossed the tracks that led to the Yankees' huge depot. He'd known there would be changes on the riverfront, but he never could have imagined this.

Edward followed the others up the steps to the top of the bluff and stood staring at the rows of cabins that stretched as far as he could see. His skin crawled. This didn't seem like home at all! Even the ground under his feet felt different. He looked down and saw that mud churned by soldiers' boots had baked brick-hard in the spring sun. He couldn't see a single blade of grass.

No one spoke as they walked across the barren wasteland toward the house. Edward heard Mother cry out when she opened the door, but he still wasn't prepared for what he saw inside. The front room was completely empty. Floors that had once been polished until the wood glowed were ruined by ugly water stains, and mud and trash were everywhere.

Edward wondered numbly what had become of the furniture—and of the family portraits that had hung on the walls. Even the marble mantel was gone. He could hear the echo of footsteps as the others moved from room to room while he stood staring at a long, ugly crack in the plaster beside the fireplace.

A knock at the other door made Edward's heart leap, and he fought to keep his voice steady as he called, "I'll see who it is." Filled with anticipation, he hurried through the hall. He already knew who it was, knew that special knock, that *tap, tappity-tap.* This time it wasn't his imagination—Simon was here!

But when Edward reached the door, the porch was empty except for a large cloth sack, and Simon was halfway across what had been the lawn. Staring after him, Edward felt an aching sadness. Again, Simon had left without a word.

Edward watched until the other boy disappeared between two abandoned cabins before he bent to pick up the sack, then stared in disbelief at what lay beneath it. "Father's field glasses!" He *had* left them on the tree platform, and Simon had kept them safe for him all that time. Edward's heart sang as he slipped the field glasses into the sack.

Back in the empty parlor, he slung the sack off his shoulder, ignoring the eager questions as everyone gathered around to see what was in it. He was the center of attention as he lifted out bags of sugar and white flour, a ham, cans of oysters, peaches, and condensed milk—even a bag of roasted coffee beans. A warm feeling crept over Edward. Simon had been his friend after all, and the gifts he'd left said more than words ever could have.

"But who on earth brought us all this?" Mother asked, scooping up a handful of coffee beans and breathing in the rich aroma.

"It was Simon," Edward said quietly.

"Simon! Are you sure?"

"Positive, Mother. I saw him."

"Imagine being so destitute you're forced to accept charity from somebody you used to *own,*" Duncan said bitterly.

"How can you think this is charity?" Edward protested. "All these things are luxuries! It's the dried beans and rice and salt pork we've been getting from the Yankee commissary for the past month that's charity. And another thing," he said as he reached back into the sack and pulled out the field glasses, "Simon found these and returned them. You thought he stole them, remember?"

Duncan scowled and muttered something under his breath.

Mother pressed the back of her hand to her forehead and asked, "Must you argue? Aren't things bad enough without that?"

"We're still alive, don't forget," Becky said, her voice bright. "Our whole family, and Daniel, too."

Yes, Edward thought bleakly, his anger fading, but what about Aunt Charlotte's family? What about Wesley? And Uncle Gilbert, whose "hero's death" helped buy time for the army to leave the city and postponed General Lee's surrender for a week?

"We *are* still alive," Becky repeated, "and Father should be home any day now."

"Home!" Duncan said harshly. "You call this 'home'?"

Edward felt a blinding flash of anger. "Well," he said, the words pouring out like a flood, "it's still a better home than that bombproof in the trenches where you lived before you caught a fever. That 'home' made you so sick you would have died if I hadn't gone behind the Yankee line to get the medicine you needed. Which you've never even mentioned." He stopped, stunned by the force of his own words and the tumult of feelings they unleashed, feelings he hadn't even known he had.

Duncan took a step back. "You went behind the enemy line?" Both his voice and his face showed amazement.

"I told you that, Duncan!" Mother said indignantly.

"I must have been too sick to remember." Looking at Edward as though he were seeing him for the first time, Duncan said, "I can't believe I owe my life to *you!* I always thought you were— Well, I never thought you were very brave. You were always drawing. Or reading." His voice faded away. "I, uh, I guess I was wrong. Thanks."

Still feeling unsettled after his outburst, Edward wasn't sure how to respond, but finally he said stiffly, "Mother was depending on me." He turned on his heel and headed for the veranda.

But his brother followed him outside. "Can you tell me how you did it?" Duncan asked. "And what it was like? Behind the enemy line, that is." His face had the eager expression that had been missing ever since his illness and the fall of Petersburg.

Edward felt his tension begin to drain away. "I'll tell you the whole story," he said, suddenly glad of the chance to share his adventure with someone who would appreciate it, "and then you can tell me what it was like in the trenches."

"It was awful," Duncan said quietly. "You can't begin to imagine what it was like."

Tentatively, Edward asked, "Are you sorry you went?"

Duncan shook his head. "It was something I had to do."

He hesitated a moment before he said, "You know, when the home guard held off the enemy cavalry last June, I was really proud. But the way things turned out, I guess it would have been better if the Yankees had taken Petersburg that morning and been done with it."

Edward could hardly believe that Duncan, of all people, had come right out and said what *he* had hardly dared to think. Careful to keep the surprise out of his voice, he added, "The war would have ended then, without the siege. Uncle Gilbert and Wesley would still be alive."

"And Riverview wouldn't have been completely wrecked," Duncan added bitterly.

After a moment's silence Edward said, "We'd better bring our things up from the wharf."

As the two brothers walked toward the bluff, Simon watched them from the doorway of the cabin that had been General Grant's headquarters. This was what he'd been waiting for—one last glimpse of Edward, and a chance to let Edward know that *he* was alive and well.

It had been worth the trouble, Simon decided. Worth carrying that sack of provisions from the hospital kitchen to the ruined plantation every day for the past two weeks and then carrying it back again when the packet boat didn't stop. Or when it brought only soldiers.

Gabriel hadn't understood. "An act of charity should be done in secret," he'd said. Simon had finally given up trying to explain that it was an act of friendship, not charity, and that Edward would know what it meant.

As Simon watched the brothers start down the steps to

the wharf he mused, "Must be gonna carry up whatever they brought back from Petersburg with 'em." He waited until they struggled up the last few steps with a trunk and slumped down onto it to rest. A smile spread over his face when he saw the field glasses slung across Edward's chest.

Simon was about to leave when he saw Edward glance in his direction, take a few steps toward him, and then stop uncertainly. With his eyes on the boy who had been his master, Simon slowly raised an arm in greeting.

Across the barren expanse of hardened mud, Edward clasped both hands high above his head. Simon's face broke into a smile, and he returned the gesture—their old signal that meant "I made it!" Then he turned and walked away without looking back.

Edward *had* made it, Simon thought, and so had he. His spirits soared, and he broke into a run, headed toward the hospital and Gabriel.

NOTES FOR HISTORY BUFFS

With the exception of briefly mentioned military and civilian leaders, the characters in *Across the Lines* are fictitious. Although Riverview is based on Appomattox Manor at City Point (now the historic district of Hopewell, Virginia), Edward's family bears no resemblance to the family that once owned that plantation.

United States Colored Troops were involved in all battles in which they appear in this book, but different units fought in the June 15 battle and the Battle of the Crater. (The last-minute substitution of untrained white soldiers for the well-trained Negroes after the explosion was made to prevent possible charges that the army was using the Negroes as cannon fodder.)

The Jefferson Davis quote Duncan read is from the Confederate president's July 16, 1864, meeting with Union representatives.

The Abraham Lincoln quote Gabriel read in the paper is from the president's December 6, 1864, message to Congress.

The explosion at the City Point munitions wharf was sabotage, the work of a Confederate agent, but this was not known until after the war was over.

As many as a dozen soldiers were "messmates," rather than the groups of four shown camping together in this book.

Although in this story the Confederate hospital was out of quinine, hospitals in Petersburg usually were well supplied during the siege. Medicine was often obtained from Union sources in exchange for large quantities of the tobacco stockpiled by the Confederate government.